Andrew Matthews

Andrew Matthews was born in Barry, South Wales, in 1948. He lives in Reading with his wife, Sheena, and their cats. He taught English in Yately School for many years before becoming a full-time writer in 1994. He has written many books for teenagers and younger readers. His hobbies include reading, listening to music and playing the guitar (badly). He hates travelling but likes being places. When he is nervous, he makes silly jokes. All the nice characters in his stories are based on real people – the nasty, irresponsible ones are made up.

Also in the Contents series

Contents

Seeing
in Moonlight

ANDREW MATTHEWS

mammoth

First published in Great Britain 1995 by Mammoth
Reissued 1998 by Mammoth
an imprint of Egmont Children's Books Limited
Michelin House, 81 Fulham Road, London SW3 6RB

Copyright © Andrew Matthews, 1995

The moral rights of the author and cover illustrator have been asserted.

ISBN 0 7497 1702 5

10 9 8 7 6 5 4 3 2 1

A CIP catalogue record for this title
is available from the British Library

Printed in Great Britain
by Cox & Wyman Ltd, Reading, Berkshire

For Sadie

Friendship is love without wings
Lord Byron

1

Every morning the cockerel in the chicken coop across the way from the apartment starts crowing at four forty-five. He's got such an excess of male hormones that I've christened him Testikles.

Since Testikles makes going back to sleep impossible, at five I rise and begin the day. Actually, to be honest 'rise' is a little too glamorous a verb – 'clamber' or 'drag' would be more appropriate.

I don't actually wake up until the second cup of coffee out on the balcony. There's a good view over the little valley and the olive groves, and the town, and then the sea. Most mornings I watch the sunrise. It's all pastel pinks and mauves – I never really appreciated how vulgar nature could be until I came to Greece.

I watch fishing boats sail out, making dark lines in the harbour water; I listen to the clocking of the goat-bells from the mountains behind me; somehow the time passes.

About half-nine I stroll down to the taverna,

through one of the last bits of the old village. Below the taverna the road is tarmacked and it's all neon and mini-markets. Above the taverna, old ladies in black sit in the sunshine making lace. They all wish me good day.

No matter how hot it is, the taverna's always cool because of the shade from the mulberry tree growing in the middle of it. Nikos sits in the coolest corner, doing his VAT returns and grumbling about the government. I make him a cup of Nescafé, he smokes a cigarette and we exchange the usual joke about his breakfast being a cup of coffee and a cough. He still can't say my name properly – Wayne sounds like 'Oowhine' when he says it.

I start to sweep up all the broken crockery from the wild ethnic dancing of the night before. When I first came here, I thought I was going to do wonderful pictures of the landscape, but they all turned out like Painting by Numbers. The best work I've done is a series of watercolours of smashed plates.

Georgiou comes in some time after ten and proceeds to chatter. I don't think he can speak English without flirting, no matter who he's talking to – he's such a tart. We laugh a lot. I'm supposed to be teaching him better English and he's supposed to be teaching me Greek, but all we teach one another is swear words.

Sometimes when we're laughing, it feels like I've been here for ages and I forget that the place and the people were ever new. Other times it feels as if I've only just arrived.

But all the time, I'm remembering. My body

is in Greece on auto-pilot, while the rest of me is back in a different place and a different time, when I wasn't the same person I am now. It was only two years ago, but even at the best of times there's a lot of difference between being sixteen and being going on nineteen – and two years ago it wasn't the best of times. It was just after I'd learned how useful it could be to write about myself with total honesty. Useful, but impossible. Human beings can't be honest about themselves, it's not in their nature, but watching someone being dishonest can be fascinating – especially when it's you.

Of course, what's started off all this memory thing is those letters I got last week . . .

And that's a lie. I'm not being honest. Nothing started me off remembering what happened, because I remember it every day. How could I possibly forget it? If it hadn't happened, I wouldn't be here; I wouldn't be me.

3

2

Once upon a time there were three friends and their names were Bron, Mikki and Wayne . . .

The truth is more complicated, of course, because Mikki's real name was Kim and the three of us weren't just friends once upon a time, we were friends all the time. I used to say that we'd been friends since before we were born. Or was it Bron who said it? It sounds like a Bron thing – though it could have been Mikki.

This is the problem with trying to remember. We borrowed so many of each others' thoughts that we forgot who had them first. I think back, and there are times when it's difficult to work out where one of us ended and the others began. We were the Great Triangle.

We met at primary school – that much I do remember – in the playground at North-meadows. Mikki was hanging upside-down from the top bar of the climbing frame, Bron was crouched by the side of it. I'm not sure what she was doing – probably caring for something, rescuing a ladybird or moving an ant somewhere it wouldn't get trodden on.

I already knew Bron, but I don't know what made me go over and speak to Mikki. Perhaps someone dared me, or perhaps I dared myself, but I sashayed up to the climbing frame and said, 'Raymond Bryant can see your knickers.'

Mikki managed to shrug, even though she was upside-down.

'So?' she said. 'So can you.'

'But I'm not rude,' I said. 'Raymond Bryant is rude.'

'Oh,' said Mikki, 'I'd better thump him then.'

Bron looked up at us both. I'll never forget how gentle and dismayed her eyes were.

'You're not going to hurt him, are you?' she said.

Mikki went off to find Raymond Bryant, Bron went with her to make sure no one got injured and I went with them because I'd made up my mind that they would be good friends to have: Mikki would fight to defend me and Bron would comfort me. In the end we fought for and comforted each other, but a friendship has to start for some reason, and in my case it was selfishness.

And loneliness . . .

I'd tried to be friends with the boys in my class, but they were physical and loud. They were obsessed with being better than each other and running and fighting and shouting – activities that didn't interest me at all. Bron and Mikki and I were on the same wavelength, and wavelength is precisely the right metaphor. Before I met them, there was nothing in my head but a hissing sound, like white noise; afterwards I could hear voices, speaking a language I understood.

And the voices and the understanding continued from then on.

Right from the start we knew that it was special. A lot of people make friends without noticing it's happened and they take their friends for granted. Bron, Mikki and I never did that. At the end of our first week together I wrote out a declaration of friendship and we all signed it. Mikki wanted us to sign in blood, but in the end we settled on green Biro.

We were always signing declarations and swearing oaths, as though once every so often we needed to renew the friendship. We memorised different verses of poems so that they wouldn't be complete unless we were together. I tried to cut a coin into three pieces once. I didn't get very far because I used a nail-file, but I didn't stop trying until I got a blister.

And then there was New Place.

I dream about New Place. I dream that I'm walking through the estate and then along Whitehead Road to the pylon with the buzzing cables. I jump across the dry ditch and go down the bank to the flinty path that leads to the lakes. About twenty metres down the path there's a stile in a gap in the hawthorn hedge. I climb over the stile, and I'm in New Place.

There's not much to look at: some scrubby trees, a field, a bridge over a stream – but it feels like I've come home. It always felt that way.

We never worked out which of us actually discovered New Place, or who first suggested meeting there. We nearly had an argument about it once. Mikki ended it by saying we probably used to meet there in a previous lifetime – or it could have been Bron, or I might have said it . . .

New Place became essential in Year Nine and we met there every Sunday afternoon. The hormones were going round our bodies behaving like Visigoths sacking ancient Rome. Bron and Mikki were realising that having feelings about boys was difficult and painful and I was realising that having any feelings at all was difficult and painful – especially when I tried to work out what feelings to have about whom.

We decided (with another declaration, or perhaps it was a testament) that in New Place we could say anything we liked. New Place was outside the real world, so it didn't matter what confessions we made there. What eventually happened was that New Place became so real to us that the rest of the world didn't matter.

And then things changed. I don't know why – I don't think there was a single reason and it didn't happen all at once – but there came a time when we hid things from each other, even at New Place. We went through a curious phase when we pretended that life was too complex to be truthful about.

So, in the final term of Year Eleven, we kept totally honest diaries and agreed to show them to each other.

We thought it was the most painful time in our lives, but we were wrong: it wasn't the most painful time in our lives – just one of the most confused.

What came out of all the confusion was the Great Triangle. Our various expeditions into love came to grief and we were left with each other, in a friendship that was stronger than before. We held each other up through the GCSE exams, and after the last one was over, we met in New Place and danced around, and laughed, and lay down and looked at the sky.

Bron said, 'I don't want this to stop, I want it to go on like this forever.'

Mikki said, 'Nothing and no one is ever going to touch us.'

I said, 'What about if Mr Right comes along?'

Mikki said, 'If Mr Right comes along, I'm sure Bron and I will like him too, Wayne.'

And we cackled like twigs snapping in the fire.

In New Place once, Mikki said, 'I'm a fatalist, anarchist, feminist atheist. I believe that when you die, that's it.'

Bron said, 'I think you live on through your friends and your children.'

I said, 'Art makes people immortal. When you look at a great painting, you're seeing the most important part of the painter, the part that lives forever.'

It was the kind of thing we said at New Place. At New Place nothing sounded pretentious – even when it was.

3

I've checked the dates in an old calendar: the last GCSE was on a Thursday in June and the next time the Great Triangle assembled was the following Sunday.

That Sunday began rather trickily, because over breakfast my father decided to have what he called 'a little man-to-man chat' with me. He began as casually as a grizzly bear hunting salmon.

'So, Wayne,' he said, 'now that you've completed your GCSE examinations, have you given any thought as to how you might occupy yourself this summer?'

I don't know if my father actually spoke to me like this, or whether my memories are mixed up with my feelings about him; he always seemed to talk to me as though he were delivering an after-dinner speech.

'I'm going to make a boot,' I said.

This even caught Mother's attention. She put her teacup into its saucer with such force that the china rang.

'Did you say . . . a boot, dear?' she said.

'Yes,' I said.

'A boot?' said Father.

'That's right,' I said, 'a boot.'

They couldn't have looked more astonished if I'd slapped them with a brace of halibut.

My plan was to build a giant Doc Marten's boot with chicken wire and papier mâché. It was going to be a statement: any everyday object becomes strange and ridiculous if you scale it up large enough. The boot was meant to show people that reality was totally crazy if you looked at it in the right way.

'It's going to be about two metres high – a black boot,' I said.

Father's tongue moved around his teeth, searching for words.

'But . . . why?' he said.

'Because it isn't there,' I said.

'Because what isn't there?' he said.

It wasn't Father's lack of understanding that irritated me, so much as the *way* he didn't understand: the *is-it-me?* frown, the eyes rolling around, the clearing of his throat as though he were clearing away the problem.

I gave up, because there was really no point. If I could have explained something so that Father understood it, it would have been too boring to interest me in the first place.

Father said, 'I was talking to Arthur Toynbee yesterday evening.'

He paused significantly; I considered applauding or swooning, but in the end I just said, 'Oh?'

Father said, 'There's a temporary vacancy in

11

the drawing office of his firm. He wondered if you might be interested in it . . .'

Since I'd never met Mr Toynbee in my life, it didn't seem likely that the offer had been made as nonchalantly as Father was trying to make out – Mr Toynbee had probably been the victim of some terrible Rotarian blackmail.

I saw it all. Father's plots were as difficult to take apart as Lego bricks. I wanted to be an artist: art meant drawing; architects did drawings. If I got a summer job with a firm of architects, perhaps I'd forget about wanting to be an artist and be inspired to want something more sensible.

'Is the pay good?' I asked.

'Oh, we didn't discuss that sort of thing,' said Father, 'but I've thought of something you might consider investing in.'

I said, 'Oh?'

'Boxing lessons,' said Father. 'After that thug assaulted you at the Year Prom, it would be just as well if you learned how to take care of yourself.'

'It wasn't a thug, it was Geoff Stevens and it was all a stupid mistake,' I said. 'What's the matter, don't *you* want to take care of me any more?'

Father's sense of humour was somewhat underdeveloped and this last quip was not well received. Father believed that he was acting in my best interests and I believed he was trying to turn me into a clone. We had words and Mother became anxious – but then Mother became anxious about everything. She

12

got stressed-out when she loaded the dish-washer.

In the end I compromised for the sake of some peace. I agreed to take the job, but I declined the boxing lessons. I told Father I'd learn how to run. He took me seriously . . .

After lunch, I walked to New Place. The arrangement was that we should each go by a different route to avoid meeting on the way. If there was an accidental encounter, we weren't to say anything, because talk outside New Place might not be entirely honest. Inside New Place you could trust 'hello' to be real and not merely polite.

It wasn't a very inspiring walk, visually. The estate always struck me as looking spilled rather than planned. It was a hot day – unusual for late June. Generally when the exams finished, blazing heat and high pollen-counts were replaced by cold winds and torrential rain – but that day was so hot that the tarmac on Locke Road pavement had gone as soft as fudge.

When I got to New Place, Mikki was already there. She was in her black leather jacket and blue jeans and she was leaning on the bridge looking down into the stream. Then she noticed I was there and ran towards me, as nervous and leggy as a colt.

'Guess what?' she said.

'What?'

'Guess!' she said.

'I give up.'

'Suze is going out on her first date!' said Mikki.

13

'My God!' I said. 'How old is she?'

'Thirteen.'

'They grow up fast!' I said.

It was very depressing – Suzanne was a toddler when I first met her, and now she was thirteen. I wondered where all the time had gone.

'Who's the lucky guy?' I said.

Mikki did this strange hopping movement around me – the Dance of the Sugar Plum Kangaroo, perhaps. It was a typical Mikki displacement-activity.

'Is it someone with zits and a greasy quiff?' I asked. 'Oh, I do hope so!'

'It's Dave Allbright,' said Mikki.

'Ah, yes,' I said. 'He's in Year Ten, isn't he? Didn't you once say—'

'Yes! Yes, all right, I fancy him!' said Mikki. 'He's a year younger than I am, but I fancy him. What's the matter, have you got some kind of a problem with that?'

'No,' I said, 'I just—'

But Mikki wasn't in listening mode. I could tell that something was wrong and that she was talking loudly about something else to try and drown it out.

'My kid sister's going out with someone I fancy when *I* don't get to go out with someone I fancy! That's just like so bloody typical! There she is, on the verge of starting her sex-life and here I am in my old leather jacket!'

Mikki was always dancing. Even her words danced. I watched her pretending to be angry to get rid of her anger and I could see that

14

the real problem wasn't Suzanne, it was herself.

'She asked me how far she should go on the first date!'

I said, 'What did you tell her – down to Safeways and back?'

'Then she asked me if she should let him cop a feel!' said Mikki. 'Imagine, my kid sister asking me questions like that!'

'The strumpet!' I said. 'What does your father think of it all?'

This was no light-hearted question, since Mikki's father was at an awkward age. He'd recently turned forty and didn't like to be reminded of it. Suze going out on her first date was just the sort of thing that might remind him.

'Suze got me to tell him,' Mikki said.

'I hope you were gentle with him,' I said.

'Of course I was,' said Mikki. 'I said, *Hey, Suze has got a date but she's too chicken to tell you about it.*'

'And how did he react?'

'He took it like an adult,' said Mikki. 'He played a Rolling Stones CD later on, but otherwise he was fine.'

Her eyes caught the light differently and she looked sad. Mikki saw me seeing.

'Wayne . . .' she said, and then her eyes changed. All the sadness went out of them and she smiled like a time-lapse film of a flower opening.

'Oh, look!' she said. 'There's Bron!'

4

Lovely Bron, walking across the grass and daisies with her smile in her eyes. Bron, as serene and deep as a river. She had the kind of calm that spread into you if you stayed round her.

Sometimes I think that Bron had it hardest of all: everyone expected so much of her. Teachers called her 'a natural academic' and predicted that she'd get A grades. Not many people could see the kind of pressure that put her under – being a natural anything takes a lot of practice.

Bron didn't know she was beautiful. Everybody assumed she did and that she had lots of boyfriends, but she didn't. Males were afraid of Bron, she was so gentle and caring that they saw the danger of getting too involved.

Bron cared about everything, from her little sister Ellie to endangered species, famine victims and abused children. She seemed to have the whole world on her conscience.

I got bitchy when I needed to protect myself and Mikki got angry, but Bron didn't have any defences at all. I used to look at how open she was and tremble.

We did the Incredible Hug – the one that took us into another dimension where there was no time or gravity. Inside the hug I could feel Mikki's energy spiralling into a corkscrew and Bron's black-treacle peacefulness.

I told Bron and Mikki about the conversation with my father. They both laughed at my impersonation of him, but Bron's laugh was a little reserved – she didn't care for cruel humour.

'Wayne the architect, eh?' she said. 'Will you have to dress formally?'

'Oh, yes!' I said. 'Shirt, tie and Masonic thong.'

'I've got a summer job,' said Mikki, not sounding very happy about it. 'Diana wants me to work mornings at the Hot Pot.'

I said, 'I thought you hated Diana.'

'I do,' said Mikki. 'Her voice makes me hurl.'

'I thought you hated the Hot Pot,' I said.

'I do,' said Mikki, 'but I really like the money. It means I can afford to offend my parents.'

'I don't know how you can bear it, frying up bits of dead animals,' I said.

'That's right, Wayne, be a silver-tongued devil!' said Mikki. 'I mean, I know the Hot Pot's only a skanky little greasy-spoon caff, but you make it sound like a five-star gourmet paradise.'

Bron said, 'I had a letter from my father. He wants me to stay with him in the States.'

This had much the same effect as dropping

a sheep's eye into a pool filled with piranha fish.

'Oh, wh-a-a-t?' said Mikki.

I just said, 'Oh,' because I couldn't think what to say. The thought of the summer without Bron put me in a little panic.

Mikki said, 'Tell him to naff off! You don't owe him anything! Anyway, you can't go. You're one side of the triangle. Without you there'll just be an angle.'

I said, 'There's more to life than being a side, Mikki.'

We sat down on the grass and talked. New Place was used to our voices and it felt all right to talk there.

Bron said, 'I always blamed Dad for him and Mum breaking up. Because he walked out on us, I thought it was his fault; but since I found out that Mum was just as much to blame, I've been feeling . . .'

'Guilty?' I suggested.

'I suppose so,' said Bron.

Mikki got angry at this. Mikki was very impressive when she was angry. Rage made her light up like a flame.

'That's just crap!' she said. '*They* made a mess of things and *you* feel guilty about it?'

'I feel guilty because of the way I thought about Dad,' said Bron. 'I used to think he was cold and selfish and I tried hard not to love him because I thought he didn't love me. Now I don't know what to think. I need to spend some time with him to find out.'

I knew there was more to it than that. Bron

needed time to sort out how she felt about her mother's plans to remarry. Somewhere deep inside Bron there was still a little girl who dreamed that one day her mother and father would get back together and she had to find a way of saying goodbye to her.

They say that your first seven years influence the rest of your life, but that's wrong. Everything that happens influences the rest of your life, it's just that some things are more obvious than others.

Bron looked at the darkness in Mikki's face and said, 'It'll only be three weeks. You'll hardly notice I've gone.'

Mikki said, 'Since we were six years old the longest we've been apart is nine days. I'll notice you've gone.'

I said, 'You've got to go.'

Bron looked at me and I could see that she knew what I meant, so I tried to lighten things up a little. I said, 'Think of the burgers – and Disney World!'

Bron said, 'Dad lives in Washington.'

I said, 'I *meant* Washington.'

But I couldn't really raise the gloom that Bron's news had cast over the afternoon.

When we left New Place, Mikki walked part of the way with me.

She said, 'She'll be all right, won't she? Only America's so dangerous.'

I said, 'Everywhere's dangerous, Mikki. The roof could fall in on you while you're lying in bed tonight. Worrying won't stop it happening.'

'I don't know what I'd do if anything happened to Bron,' Mikki said.

'You'd be upset for ever,' I said. 'That's the risk you take when you care about someone. Eventually you'd find a way of carrying on with your life. It's what everybody does. There's nothing else to be done.'

'When you get right down to it, you're just a sentimental fool, aren't you? said Mikki.

I don't know why sarcasm is supposed to be the lowest form of wit.

5

At Toynbee, Charles & Wooton Ltd, I drew pipes. Not with a pencil and paper, you understand. The only pencil I ever saw in the place was used to keep a window open. At TC&W, 'drawing' meant using computers. I didn't even have to use a graphics program, I just had to select predrawn sections of piping and insert them on to a prepared background to produce a working design. I never did find out what it was a working design of. It might have been part of a factory – no one bothered to say – but as far as giving me any kind of pleasure or satisfaction, I'd rate it on a par with banging my head against a brick wall – all the pleasure came when I stopped.

The premises were impressive – a tobacco-coloured block of tinted-glass and steel, with so many potted plants in the foyer that it resembled one of the unspoiled reaches of the Amazon – but it was staffed with people who didn't seem to know what they were doing. And their clothes! They all wore polyester next to their skins. I think perhaps some sort of drab contest was going on that nobody told me about. I discovered that the further up the organisation one went, the more intense the confusion and drabness became.

On my first day, I encountered Mr Toynbee himself, wearing a suit that looked as if it had been woven from navel-fluff. He leaned into the office and smiled at me with his teeth.

'Ah!' he said, 'It's . . . um . . . er . . . ?'

'Yes, that's right,' I said.

'Good!' said Mr Toynbee. 'And is everything . . . um . . . er . . . ?'

'Oh, yes,' I said.

'Good!' said Mr Toynbee. 'Then I'll, ah, leave you to . . . um . . . er . . .'

'I'll get right on it,' I said, thinking that here was a man with enough letters after his name to make a hand at Scrabble.

I came to realise that Father's plan wasn't going to work and that the world of the architect's office wasn't for me, but it took time – about twenty seconds. I didn't understand that kind of work and I still don't. How can people devote their lives to such time-consuming and unfulfilling occupations? Don't they care? Are they stupid? Can't they see?

Here on the island, work is a laid-back thing. Nothing much happens until the evening, when the tourists arrive. Wine makes their faces soften, and they laugh. We light the candles and people look good. There's flirtation, and banter, and everybody is relaxed.

I have free time mid-afternoon, when the sun's like a migraine. That's when I do the other work, the work I do for myself. I probably take painting less seriously than I used to, but it's more important to me because I'm getting better at putting myself in the pictures.

At TC&W, lunchtimes kept me sane. I used to take my sandwiches to Russell Park – not one of the world's great beauty-spots, admittedly, but at least the flowerbeds weren't grey and I could feed breadcrusts to the sparrows. I'd found an excellent book of extremely depressing Japanese poetry and I used to sit in the sunshine reading it, thinking what a tragically misunderstood person I was . . . and I was.

There was no Japanese poetry the first Wednesday at Toynbee, Charles & Wooton, though, because when I left the building at lunchtime, I found Mikki waiting for me. She looked pale and agitated and she'd tucked her hair behind her ears, a sure sign that she wanted to talk.

And she wanted to talk about Nick.

There was no preamble. Mikki favoured the parachute-jump approach and words came tumbling out of her like sky-divers. We walked down the street, crossed the road, went into Russell Park and Mikki talked the whole way. She talked us on to a park bench and through half my sandwiches.

Nick was a university student with a vacation job at the Hot Pot. Mikki went into work one morning and found him in the yard at the back of the café. He was standing next to some dustbins, crying. Mikki naturally did what any well-balanced and sensible person wouldn't have done: she cuddled him and he talked.

He'd been involved with a girl at university and she'd just written to him to end it.

'D'you know what she put?' Mikki said. 'She put – *I don't know where you're going in life, but I don't think you're going there with me.* I mean, what a crap thing to write to someone!'

I said something about it having all the sincerity of an awards ceremony.

Mikki said, 'And suddenly it's like – POW! I'm an agony aunt and I'm giving him advice. You'd figure a nineteen year-old university student would have it all sussed!'

I said, 'What did you say?'

'The usual sort of stuff,' said Mikki. 'I told him there were plenty more fish in the sea and he said he didn't want to go out with a fish and then we both started laughing.'

The fish became a private joke between them, and then because they had a private joke they had a relationship, and then . . .

'And then?' I said.

'And then this morning, he asked me out,' said Mikki.

She didn't look pleased when she said it, she looked troubled. Her mouth was turned down at the corners.

'I gather you said no,' I said.

'You know what?' said Mikki. 'I was scared. I mean, I wasn't scared of Nick or anything, it was just the idea of getting involved with someone again made me panic.'

'Because of Bryan?' I said.

Mikki didn't answer; she didn't have to – of course it was because of Bryan.

Mikki said, 'I told Nick he was a mate. I mean, I know males and females can be friends without any sexual thing, but . . .'

'But what?'

It was like watching a horse in a show-ring making up its mind whether to jump or refuse. Mikki took a deep breath and said, 'I want to believe in the perfect bloke. I want to believe there's someone out there who's just right for me in the same way as I'm just right for him, and as soon as we meet, we'll know.'

I said, 'So what's stopping you?'

She said, 'Bryan bloody Eaves! How can I trust anyone again?'

She meant how could she trust herself again.

I said, 'Is that what was worrying you last Sunday?'

Mikki laughed and shook her head. Her hair came untucked and fell across her face.

'You're amazing, Wayne! How did you know I was worried last Sunday?'

I said, 'Because I'm Amazing Wayne.'

Mikki said, 'I'm getting these weird phone-calls. When I answer, the person on the other end hangs up.'

She used her no-big-deal voice, which meant that she was anxious.

'Who have you told?' I said.

'No one.'

I said, 'Mikki!'

She said, 'It happened before. When Dad and that woman from his office had that thing, she used to ring him and put the phone down if anyone else answered. I'm frightened it's happening again and Mum will find out.'

Mikki gave me her pain. I put a frame around it and gave it back to her. I told her that she wasn't thirteen any more and there was no need to protect her parents, so she should tell them about the phone calls and after that it was up to them.

I didn't say anything about trusting. How could I? I was afraid of trusting people myself. I didn't even know what I wanted to trust them with.

We spent a lot of time being frightened – mostly of what other people might think of us. It never occurred to us that other people weren't thinking about us at all.

I said, 'It wouldn't have worked out with Nick anyway. Nick and Mikki has got too much alliteration in it.'

I remember her laughing, and how I thought that making her laugh was the best feeling there was. She leaned her head against my shoulder and held on to my arm. Anybody who saw us would have thought we were a couple, when really we were a hermit-crab and a shell.

6

I've always been an outsider, an observer; I think artists have to be. You have to stand apart from what happens to you and see how a picture might be made from it. I watch people laughing, or crying, or being angry and a part of my mind is thinking about how I could best catch them in paint. No matter how much emotion I'm feeling, there's something inside me that isn't feeling at all – it's watching and thinking, 'Can I do anything with this? Is this any good?' I don't know if I'm using it, or its using me.

A time of pictures, then . . .

That evening before Bron went away, the dusk was grey-blue. The Great Triangle sauntered through if, knowing a goodbye had to come but not wanting it and not knowing how to say it. We were used to meeting and looking pleased to see each other but we had no real experience of parting.

We couldn't remember if the States was ahead or behind in time. We worked it out using Mikki as the world and me as the sun. It was stupid and we laughed, but after we stopped laughing we fell into a hole of silence and things felt as though they might become too real to handle.

Mikki said, 'Will you write?'

'Of course,' said Bron.

Mikki said, 'How long do letters take?'

I said, 'It depends on how much you've got to say.'

'I didn't mean that!' said Mikki. She turned to Bron and said, 'Will you phone?'

Bron said, 'If I can.'

Then Mikki said, 'You are coming back, aren't you?'

It was a good question. It had occurred to me but I hadn't found the right time to ask it. I'd built a chain of ifs into the future: if Bron got on with her father, and if she really couldn't accept the idea of her mother and Steve, and if she enjoyed the American life style . . .

Mikki said, 'Don't let anything happen to you. I mean, you mustn't have an accident, or get mugged.'

Bron said, 'If you say so.'

Mikki said, 'I want you to come back already and you haven't gone yet.'

'If Bron were to leave before she arrived,' I said, 'then she'd be back before she left.'

Bron said, 'Is there anything you want me to get you?'

'A really gross T-shirt,' said Mikki.

'A black baseball-cap,' I said.

And there's a picture: three young people at

the corner near Mikki's house. Bron is smiling her warm smile, Mikki has her arms held out, modelling the invisible T-shirt and I'm standing with my hands in my pockets, shoulders slightly hunched, trying to make myself look smaller – trying not to exist. Behind us, the pale houses are glowing in the twilight; above us, a sky filled with darkness is about to fall.

I said, 'Don't you dare come back with an American accent.'

Mikki said, 'Send rude postcards.'

Bron said, 'I'm going to miss you two.'

'We know,' I said.

'If I didn't say it, you might not be sure,' said Bron.

Mikki didn't say anything because she was too upset. Bron and I walked her to her house. She hugged us both and went inside.

As we walked away, Bron put her arm through mine and rested her head on my shoulder.

'Have you seen anything of Geoff?' I said.

'No,' she said.

'I feel rather guilty about that,' I said. 'If he hadn't attempted to rearrange my face, I think that you and he might have got together.'

I'd tried hard enough. Bron had eaten her heart out over Geoff for almost two years and I'd tried to matchmake. Unfortunately I hadn't taken my own feelings into consideration because I hadn't realised that they were there to be considered.

Bron said, 'I loved Geoff, Geoff loved Mikki, Mikki loved Bryan, Bryan loved me. People

29

always fall in love with the wrong people and make a mess of it.'

'Like your mother and father,' I said.

'Yes,' said Bron. 'I don't believe in that kind of love any more. I don't think it's possible. I think friendship with sex is the best you can hope for.'

I wasn't so fussy about what kind of love I believed in – though I was fussier than I am now. Back then there seemed to be a bewildering variety of possibilities and I felt like a raindrop on the top of a windowpane, waiting to trickle.

Bron said, 'Will you take care of Mikki?'

'Yes,' I said.

'Will you take care of you?' said Bron.

'Mikki and I will take care of one another,' I said.

Bron said, 'If I think of you late on Sunday evening, you'll be in New Place. Will you think about me?'

'If I say yes, does it mean that I've invented the rhetorical answer?' I said.

Her cool, smooth hair brushed against my cheek.

'You understand why I've got to go, don't you?' said Bron.

'Yes,' I said.

Bron said, 'Sometimes I think you understand me better than I understand myself.'

'Oh, that's all right,' I said, 'I understand *me* better than I understand myself.'

We walked a few more close, friendly steps and I felt the time come right.

'Bron,' I said, 'are you going to come back?'

'I don't know,' she said.

I said, 'That means you might not.'

Bron said, 'I know. Mum, Steve and Ellie are so complete. They're so happy. Sometimes when I'm with them, I feel like . . .'

'An outsider,' I said.

'D'you understand everything?' said Bron.

'No,' I said, 'only being an outsider.'

'I thought parents acted for the best,' said Bron. 'I thought adults knew what they were doing – I thought they were in control.'

'No one's in control because no one knows what's going to happen,' I said.

Bron had grown up believing that she should be like her mother when she didn't actually know what her mother was like. When she'd discovered that Ellie was the product of her mother's extra-marital affair, Bron had felt betrayed and hurt and she wanted to hurt back by leaving home and going to America.

At her front door, Bron hugged me so tightly that it was difficult to breathe. She was hugging me hard just in case it was the last time and she might have been crying, but I can't be certain because she turned away and went in before I could see her face.

On the way home, the streetlamps came on, glowing red before they flickered into yellow.

And that's another picture – a solitary figure walking along a pavement. The streetlamps look like tall, slender creatures, bending their necks down to stare with their red eyes.

31

That's me, walking away from Bron's house, realising that changes were going to take place. We couldn't go on being as close as we were, because if we did then there wouldn't be room for anyone else in our lives.

7

Time goes very quickly when you're doing something you enjoy; in the dentist's chair or the shopping queue, time can slow down until a few minutes seem like a lifetime.

And then there's Toynbee, Charles and Wooton time . . .

I forget which ancient Greek was punished with having to push a millstone up a hill only to lose his grip at the top so it rolled all the way back down again, but I think he had a hand in designing the work schedules at TC&W. I disappeared into a peculiar limbo where I once caught myself believing that getting pipes into the right place on a computer screen actually mattered.

I got the first postcard from Bron about a week after she left. It was a wonderful picture of the US President done in a sort of 3D effect, so that when you moved the card he appeared to wave. On the back, Bron had written, 'AMERICA IS BIG', which appealed to the surrealist me, but of course that's why she wrote it.

Father was delighted that I'd received a postcard. He called it, 'A missive from your young lady.'

'Bron isn't my yong lady,' I told him, 'she's my friend.'

Father said, 'What's the difference?'

He said it roguishly and with a nauseating twinkle in his eye.

For a moment I considered pointing out the difference to him, but it was only for a moment.

Actually, Wayne the Friend of Females turned out to be in demand that day, because at five to five I happened to glance out of the office window and I saw Suzanne in the street below. She walked out of view, and then back into view a few moments later and I could tell she was hanging about, hoping to see me.

At five o'clock I was magically transformed from a computer accessory to something approaching a human being, and I left TC&W as fast as I could without actually breaking into a run.

I'd only taken a few steps along the street when a hand touched my shoulder. I turned and saw Suzanne.

'Suzanne!' I said, which was brilliant – not for its originality, but for the feigned surprise. 'What are you doing here? Shouldn't you be somewhere else?'

Suzanne said, 'I thought it was you!'

I didn't think about this in any depth because who else it might have been offered too much scope for flights of fancy.

It was obvious that Suzanne had something on her mind, but I didn't let on that I knew.

'Are you on your way home?' I said. 'I'll walk with you.'

It was a sticky day, but Suzanne managed to look cool and enchanting. I'd like to pretend that some of the heads that turned as we walked along were looking at me, but they were all for Suzanne.

'Wayne,' she said, 'is it all right if I talk to you?'

I said, 'I don't know. Is there a rule book we can look it up in?'

Suzanne smiled dutifully, then said, 'I mean, do you mind if I talk to you?'

'No,' I said.

What she meant was, since I was officially Mikki's friend, did I mind her poaching in her sister's preserves. How could I have minded? A large part of my defence-strategy was to surround myself with as many attractive females as I could.

Suzanne told me about her date with Dave Allbright, and how Mikki had made fun of her, and how her parents had been really nervous but had pretended not to be, and how difficult it had been to choose an outfit . . .

Her words burst in the air around me like anti-aircraft shells; I flew on steadily, dropping, 'A-ha!' and 'U-hu!' in the right places.

Dave was on time and all smiles. He was quiet and shy at first, but as they neared the doors of the Youth Club disco, he began to open up and talk, and then . . .

'It was pathetic!' said Suzanne. 'A couple of his mates turned up and one of them smuggled in a bottle of cider and they got all loud and pretended to be drunk. They were stupid.'

'That's boys for you,' I said. 'They show off when they're in packs.'

'I know Dave's really good-looking, but he's so immature,' said Suzanne.

'Boys are always immature,' I said, 'and the better-looking they are, the more immature they are.'

'Then why bother with them?' said Suzanne.

'I don't, I said.

Suzanne laughed because she thought I was telling a joke, which I was, but I was also telling the truth.

'Mikki doesn't give me any advice about boys,' Suzanne said.

'Perhaps she doesn't know much about them,' I said.

'She got off with Bryan though, didn't she? Funny they broke up so suddenly,' said Suzanne.

She was dredging for information, but I didn't give her any. I knew better than to get caught in the cross-fire between sisters.

I can't remember what I ended up saying to Suzanne, but I was touched that she'd turned to me. I had a vision of Suzanne's and Mikki's daughters coming to me for advice, and then their daughters' daughters, until I was transformed into some family totem-figure, Grandaddy Wayne. Whatever I told her, it left her laughing and feeling that whatever was wrong wasn't her fault, which is the point of exchanging confidences. Unfortunately I haven't got anyone who can do the same job for me, but I live in hope.

I think it was the following Saturday that I bumped into Bron's family – literally, actually, because I was just about to go into Barkers for a new set of brushes, when I was rugby-tackled by a small child. It was Ellie, and when I looked around I saw Steve and Bron's mother. The air prickled with awkwardness – I could see them remembering that I knew all about Ellie's parentage.

'Oh, hello, Wayne,' Bron's mother said. 'How are you?'

'I'm fine,' I said.

'Good,' she said.

'How are you?' I said.

'I'm fine,' she said, turning to Steve. 'We're both fine, aren't we?'

Steve nodded at Ellie and said, 'The three of us are fine.'

While we awaited nominations for this dazzling dialogue, Ellie stopped the circulation in my thighs with a death-lock and shouted, 'Wayneywayneywayney!'

Steve said, 'Heard anything from Bronia?'

I said, 'A postcard. She's fine.'

'She wrote to us saying everything was fine,' said Bron's mother.

'That's super,' I said. I don't know what made me say it – I just wanted to fill a silence because what we were saying to each other between the words was loud and uncomfortable.

Bron's mother touched Ellie's shoulder and said, 'Come on, Trouble! Let's buy you that milk-shake.'

Ellie looked up at me, wrinkled her nose and said, 'Strawberry!'

The way she said it made me laugh, and a wave of what might have been paternal feeling passed through me.

Steve said, 'You go on ahead. I just want to chat to Wayne for a bit.'

Bron's mother looked unhappy about this, but she steered Ellie off towards McDonald's.

'Wayne,' said Steve, 'd'you know what Bronia's plans are?'

I could have acted dumb, but what would have been the point? He was asking me if she was coming back from America, which meant that he was asking me whether she accepted him or not. I knew what he meant, and he knew I knew, and I knew he knew I knew, like a candle-flame reflected in parallel mirrors.

I said, 'As far as I know, she's coming back at the end of August.'

Steve said, 'Her father wrote to us. He wants her to live with him. He says he can give her a lot of advantages. He says there are lots of opportunities over there for someone like Bron.'

His voice was flat, but I could hear the anger in it. Steve looked at me as though he badly needed an ally.

'The bastard,' I said.

Steve smiled with relief.

'I couldn't agree more,' he said. 'Look, Wayne, if Bronia tells you anything—'

'I'll let you know at once,' I said.

'We miss her,' Steve said.

I felt sorry for him. If Bron didn't come back, her mother might blame him for it; if she did come back, he was going to be a stepfather.

'The whole world misses Bron,' I said.

Being without friends is lonely, but straightforward. When you take on friends, you take on their foibles, their fantasies and their families. What you thought was a simple connection suddenly turns into a web of responsibilities. My duties now extended to Suzanne and Steve, but I didn't mind. I thought I was detached and separate and that I could handle it all.

8

The person I was filling in for at Toynbee, Charles and Wooton returned on the Wednesday before the GCSE results came out. The other people I worked with went through the usual office rituals of buying me cream-cakes in the coffee-break and wishing me luck, but I could tell that they didn't know what to make of me. If I'd been two-dimensional and on a Paintbox menu they could have dealt with me; as it was, they gave me The Look, which I've been getting all my life.

You get The Look if you won't fit into any of the categories that people think in. If you're not handsome, or pretty, or you're not interested in dirty jokes or sport, you get The Look. Sometimes you get it when you say what you really think, but you mostly get it when people can't define you. First it disturbs them, then it irritates them; the irritation has always been the part that I enjoyed most.

Father began as soon as I got back from work. He sat me down in the lounge and poured me half a glass of medium-dry sherry, which made the whole occasion taste of Christmas.

'Well, Wayne,' Father said.

'Tolerably,' I said.

Father gave me his non-understanding expression.

'Tolerably what?' he said.

'Well,' I said.

Father moistened his lips with sherry and tried again.

'The GCSE results are out on Friday,' he said.

Didn't I just know it? The thought of it was patrolling the back of my mind like a hungry shark.

'Oh, so they are,' I said, just casually enough to make Father turn pink.

'Now that you've seen something of the wider world, I was wondering if you might have changed your mind about your A level courses,' he said.

'No,' I said.

Father grew bolder as the sherry fired his blood.

'You don't even have to stay on at school at all, you know,' he said. 'All it would take is a word to the wise – I mean, I left school when I was fifteen.'

I wanted to say, 'Yes – and look at you!'

I wanted to say, 'What was so thrilling about your life that you want me to live it over again?'

What I said was, 'I want to take my A levels,

41

go to university, get a degree and then work as a commercial artist.'

The commercial-artist idea was a new one and it wasn't so much a fib as a downright lie, but it was the sort of thing that kept Father quiet.

'And this . . . friend of yours who wrote to you from America, is that serious?' he said.

'There's no need to take out a second mortgage for my dowry quite yet,' I said.

I expected him to get angry, but he laughed.

'That's right, my boy, play the field!' he said.

I wondered which field.

Plans had been made for the day of the GCSE results. As soon as they came in the post, Bron and Mikki and I were going to take them to New Place and not look at them until the Great Triangle was assembled. I was going to open Bron's envelope, Mikki was going to open mine and Bron was going to open Mikki's. Then we were going to celebrate or commiserate. Bron's absence spoiled the original plan, but Mikki and I decided to go ahead anyway.

The envelope fluttered through the letter box at 8.15. I grabbed it off the mat and slipped outside like an eloper. I paused to pick a red carnation from the flowering border in the front garden, then I was out through the front gate and off.

I remember feeling annoyed that my future had arrived in a cheap buff envelope. I'd envisaged something more along the lines of a gilt-edged roll of vellum. As I walked, I kept touching the envelope with my fingertips and wondering what it said on the paper inside.

I had two big fears: the first was that I'd have to take full responsibility for the results because they were all my own work; the second, bigger fear was that I might be average. None of my plans included living an average life.

New Place was very clear that morning. Time had stopped. New Place got on with what it had always done – the stream flowed, bees fumbled around inside the flowers and swallows screeched overhead. Nature seemed so unhurried and calm that I was about to come over all Cosmic Hippie Wayne when Mikki arrived. She grabbed my hands and danced me round in circles and we fell over in a heap and there was no Mikki or Wayne, there was just us without Bron.

I said, 'What was the dance for?'

Mikki said, 'To stop feeling frightened.'

'Frightened of what?' I said.

Mikki broke the sky into pieces with her laugh and I gave her the red carnation.

'What's this for?' she said.

I said, 'A rose would have been too romantic. Carnations are a symbol of love without sex.'

'Are they?' said Mikki.

'Yes,' I said. 'I've just made it up.'

Mikki smelled the carnation and smiled at me.

'You're so sweet,' she said.

I said, 'Don't get soppy. I also picked it because I knew it would annoy Father. Are we going to do the exam-results thing now?'

'Yes,' said Mikki.

She looked so young as we exchanged envelopes that it made me think about the day we first met.

The results were all As, Bs and Cs. They were what we'd hoped for and we didn't know whether to laugh or cry, so we did both at the same time.

We hugged, and inside the hug Mikki said, 'I'm proud of you.'

I said, 'I'm proud of me. I'm proud of you, too. You couldn't have done it without me.'

'Tell me about it!' said Mikki. 'And you couldn't have done it without me.'

'I know,' I said. 'How can we say thanks?'

Mikki said, 'On New Year's Eve, Two Thousand, we'll have dinner together in Paris.'

'You're on,' I said. 'You buy the champagne and I'll pay for the vegeburgers.'

We walked to school to find out Bron's results. Mikki giggled at the sight of teachers in jeans and trainers, but when we checked the computer sheets, she stopped laughing.

'Seven As and two Bs?' she said. 'Being beautiful and a good mate just isn't good enough for Bron, is it?'

We felt triumphant – I think it's the only time I've had the feeling. We'd got ourselves into personal messes, but we'd come through with good exam grades and it felt as though we'd proved something to somebody.

Mikki and I went to sit on the front lawn for a while and we saw the Lush Gang cruising through. Phil Mason had his arm around Ruth Critch and Carol Miles was draped around Tony Birch's neck.

Mikki said, 'They're such decent-looking kids, aren't they? I mean, they look just like parents want kids to look.'

I said, 'How tragic, then, that Phil should be a complete slut and that Ruth has a mind like a soft-porn movie.'

Mikki said, 'You reckon Carol and Tony are doing it?'

I said, 'Yes, and it involves spawn.'

It's so easy to make cruel remarks at the expense of others – and it's so much fun.

Tony gave us his American-soap-star wave and said, 'Well, well, it's Wayne and Mikki.'

'Thanks for the confirmation, Tone,' I said, though sarcasm was wasted on Tony – as was oxygen.

'Going up the Duke tonight?' Tony said. 'The gang'll be there getting pissed-up.'

'You make it sound like a must,' I said.

After the Lush Gang left, Mikki said, 'Are you really going up the Duke tonight?'

I said, 'Why not?'

Mikki shrugged.

'It doesn't seem very you,' she said.

'And what is?' I said.

The really good questions don't have answers.

9

One day, I'll do a painting of the Duke. It'll be like one of those mediaeval pictures, so filled with figures that something's happening wherever you look. Lots of people went to the Duke because it was one of the few places where young people could meet together and chat freely. It was also incredibly easy to get served if you were under-age.

I doubt if anyone went there for the ambience. The colour scheme was cream and dark brown. Above the ersatz-brick fireplace hung a cartwheel whose worm-holes may have been genuine. On various shelves and in various niches about the place were antique plates and tankards – some of them dating right back to the 1960s. The ceiling was stained by years of cigarette-smoke.

When Mikki and I arrived, a few people from our Year were there, including the Lush Gang. Tony Birch was standing at the bar looking totally gobsmacked.

I said, 'What's wrong, Tone?'

Tony said, 'I asked for a Mexican beer with

a slice of lime in the neck. I got a lager and lime.'

'Very trendy,' I said. 'It's post-modernist rustic chic.'

Tony gave me The Look just before Mikki slapped him on the back and his drink slopped over his hand.

'Who cares, as long as it gets you out of your face?' said Mikki, and she was right.

I bought her a vodka and orange and had a pint of bitter myself. Mikki made a face when she saw it.

'You gone off cider?' she said.

I said, 'It's part of my A level-student image. Cider and lager-top are a little laddish. Best bitter suggests a more mature and stable attitude.'

'Horses have a manure and stable attitude,' said Mikki.

'Better leave the jokes to me,' I said.

She told me how her parents had reacted to her GCSE results.

'My dad hugged me,' she said. 'It made me feel like I was little again.'

'What did your mum say?' I said.

'She said she hoped I didn't make any of the mistakes she made,' said Mikki. 'I had to remind her that *I* was one of the mistakes she made. What did your parents say?'

I said, 'Father poured me a sherry and Mother took a double dose of royal jelly and got high. It must have been fully five minutes before Father started tutting over the C grades.'

For half an hour it was pure, delicious nonsense – just Mikki and I and laughter. Meanwhile, the pub filled up and got louder. New arrivals were greeted with cheers – mostly mocking and malicious, I'm pleased to say. Various people staggered over to our table to slur a few words. Dean Welldale lifted Mikki out of her chair and kissed her. Mikki wasn't flattered. She said that Dean was so drunk he would have kissed a camel if it had been wearing lipstick. I said it probably explained why he was with Donna Farron.

I had a second pint of beer and my memory is foggy after that. I've never had a good head for alcohol. I remember an extremely drunken Clive Aylott telling Mikki that he'd always fancied her, but had never had the nerve to ask her out.

'I'm glad,' said Mikki. 'One of my rejections can really hurt.'

And I remember a trip to the Gents, because on the way back I saw Geoff Stevens. He was sitting with some cronies. He turned and saw me. I know wolves don't have dark eyes, but Geoff had eyes like a wolf. He looked away as soon as our gazes met. He probably felt embarrassed. I don't know how I was feeling. I was relieved he wasn't staying on into the Sixth Form, but seeing him unexpectedly gave me a shock of fear – or was it excitement? Both, perhaps . . .

Anyway, there wasn't much opportunity to dwell on my feelings because as I got back to the table, the door opened and in came Katie

Fairlight, with Bryan Eaves on her arm – Miss Intellectual Pygmy and the Smooth King. They received a tremendous cheer, as though people were surprised that they were together. I think their relationship was fated from the start because they shared a similar view of life – amoeboid. Katie's customary smirk was smugger than usual. Bryan looked uneasy. I could tell that going out with Katie wasn't as satisfying as long-distance lusting after her. He had the air of someone who'd bitten off less than he could chew.

Then he saw Mikki, and his eyes went lost and pleading, and I saw Mikki's shoulders sag and I knew that she was hurting. Bryan had been her dream-man for over a year and she still wasn't quite awake. Mikki responded to her feelings in her typically deeply-considered way by getting completely rat-arsed.

An hour and a half later we were outside the Duke. Mikki was careering round and I kept nudging her off the road on to the grass verge.

'He's a complete and utter bastard!' she said.

I said, 'Yes, Mikki.'

She said, 'After we'd been to bed, he told me he was in love with Bron and he said he felt, like, really guilty about taking advantage of me.'

I said, 'Yes, I know, Mikki.'

She said, 'Then how come he's bonking Katie Fairlight?'

'Perhaps she's good at it,' I said.

I didn't see anything to cry over in this speculation, but the alcohol in Mikki did. She burst into tears, and I held her. Holding Mikki was always a surprise because she felt so small. Perhaps it was because when I looked at her, I saw how important she was to me.

She said, 'I thought it had gone. I thought I was over him. I thought it didn't matter.'

I said, 'Thinking doesn't have anything to do with feelings.'

She said, 'You know those paintings where if you stand up close they look a mess, but if you walk a couple of metres away you can see a cathedral, or a haystack at sunset or something?'

I said, 'Yes.'

Mikki said, 'My life's like that, only no matter how far you walk away it still looks like a mess.'

I said, 'Don't. It'll get better. You'll meet someone one day and all the waiting will have been worth it.'

'Will it?' said Mikki.

'Wait until you see in moonlight,' I said.

Mikki moved away from me and did an incredibly large blow of her nose into an incredibly small tissue.

'What does that mean?' she said.

I said, 'Places look different in moonlight. Even places you know well look mysterious and beautiful. Real love is like seeing in moonlight.'

Mikki said, 'Is it?'

I said, 'I don't know. I hope so.'

I invented all that about seeing in moonlight because I hoped it might make Mikki stop crying – and it worked; but sometimes you make things up for other people and then afterwards you find out that they're true for you, as well.

I'm still waiting to find out.

And hoping.

10

I've always been a hoarder – it must be my rodent blood. Some people have collections; I just save things – there are times when even an old sweet wrapper can be charged with significance.

Once in a while, I'll make a collage out of what I've kept – tickets, bits of travel brochures – and the collages are like pictures of my past. Of course, they're also pictures of what I considered important at the time I made them.

I've often thought of using Bron's postcards from America as part of a collage, but I've never been able to decide whether to use the pictures or the messages.

AMERICA IS BIG
MISS YOU
I AM, HOPE YOU ARE
THE WEATHER IS
SEE YOU SOONER

It was after I got the third one that I began to wonder why she wasn't writing letters, but there was only room to wonder in the back of my mind, because the front of my mind was completely occupied by Mikki.

The phone calls were still going on, and they were getting on her nerves. I tried to joke her out of it by saying that she ought to be grateful for the attention, but it wasn't really a joking matter.

She said, 'When I told my dad, I watched him carefully to see how he reacted.'

I said, 'And?'

She said, 'He looked sort of puzzled.'

'It can't have been his bimbo calling him then,' I said.

'I don't know,' said Mikki. 'He only looked sort of puzzled. I mean, I couldn't tell if he was really puzzled, or acting being sort-of puzzled because he knew that if he acted really *really* puzzled, I'd know he was acting.'

I said, 'It would be a really interesting world if people were that subtle, but it isn't, so they're not.'

The Sunday after the results, Father spoke to me. It would have been a conversation if either of us had bothered to listen. He waited until the Archers had finished, of course. The Archers habit comes to people who've reached a certain age – like the taste for beige clothes.

'Tell me, Wayne,' said Father, 'what is it that you actually do when you go out on Sundays?'

I'd been going out for two years, and he'd never asked me before; or if he had I'd fobbed him off. I'd always felt the need to keep my parents and the Great Triangle separate.

'I'm going to meet my friend Mikki,' I said.

'Who's he?' said Father.

'She,' I said.

'But Mickey is a boy's name, isn't it?'

'Mikki's real name is Kim, but she didn't like it so she turned it backwards,' I said. 'Mikki thinks it's wrong to give names to babies, because you don't know if they'll suit them when they grow up.'

Father didn't attempt to come to grips with this idea and eyebrowed it aside.

'So you've got *another* friend who's a girl?' he said.

'I believe she's of the feminine persuasion,' I said.

'I hope you're not two-timing anybody,' said Father.

He wasn't hoping anything of the kind. Wayne the Mega-Stud was an idea that greatly appealed to him.

'I'm not even one-timing anybody,' I said.

Father returned to the business section of the Sunday newspaper; he often used economics as an escape from reality.

It was overcast that day and a cool breeze was blowing. I wore black jeans and a charcoal-coloured silk bomber-jacket that I'd bought out of my ill-gotten gains from Toynbee, Charles and Wooton. It was masculine but soft and that was the kind of statement I wanted to make about myself at the time.

In New Place, I waited in the middle of the

bridge, where it wasn't water, earth or air, and where I wasn't going in any direction. Mikki arrived, and I could tell that something good had happened because her eyes were laughing. The first thing she said to me was, 'It was Bryan.'

I said, 'What was Bryan?'

'Making the phone calls,' she said.

As soon as she told me, I knew I should have known. I remembered the look that Bryan gave Mikki in the Duke and things fell into place like the tumblers of a combination-lock.

I said, 'How did you find out?'

Mikki said, 'He told me yesterday afternoon. See, Mum and Dad and Suze went shopping, and almost as soon as they'd gone, the phone started ringing. I freaked. I figured, like, if it wasn't that woman ringing my dad, then maybe it was a weirdo. I thought my life was going to turn into a teen-slash movie any minute.'

She took her fear for a walk in the world, and she wound up on the bench next to the playground on the Green. Watching the kids playing on the swings and slide calmed her down . . . and that's when Bryan sat down next to her.

While Mikki was telling me what had happened, I could see it in my imagination. Bryan expected Mikki to collapse into slush at the very sight of him; when she didn't, he smoothed his ruffled ego and fell back on to Plan B, in which he appeared as a sincere-but-misunderstood guy who was at the mercy of his passions – Mr Hormone-Victim.

Bryan told Mikki that he missed her. Katie was very attractive, but Bryan hadn't been able to talk to her in the way that he used to talk to Mikki. I was surprised to learn that he and Katie talked at all. I'd assumed that when they weren't having sex, they snorted money together.

Then Bryan really came on, in a go-for-it speech that should have had a violin accompaniment, or a soft 'dooby-wah' chorus in the background, like one of those old rock and roll records.

He'd gone out with Mikki to try and forget his obsession with Bron. He'd given no consideration to any feelings for Mikki that he might have, but after things had gone wrong between them, he'd started to think about her and then he hadn't been able to stop. He said he'd rung up, but when he heard her voice he'd been too afraid to speak.

'That's when I knew that it was him,' said Mikki. 'I mean – I've been worried sick, and scared, and I've been a total bitch to my dad, and all the time it was Bryan frigging Eaves!'

'What did you say?' I said.

'I told him to leave me alone,' said Mikki. 'That's when he said he wanted us to get back together. I mean, can you believe the guy?'

'What did you say?' I said.

'I told him to piss off. I told him I didn't want him to phone, or write, or talk to me. He looked at me, all hurt and he goes, *I thought you really cared about me, Mikki.* So I said, *I don't care about you as much as you do, Bryan, I don't think anyone ever could.'*

For three months Mikki had been like someone with a heavy pack on her back. The pack was stuffed with all her feelings about Bryan – how he'd been her ideal, how he'd manipulated her and taken advantage, how she'd been a poor victim and he'd been a mega bastard. Now she'd tipped out the pack and she could see that half the fault was hers.

'I made a mistake,' she said. 'It was just a mistake, like people are always making. It wasn't all down to Bryan at all.'

'Bryan's a spoiled child,' I said. 'He can't make up his mind what he wants, so he tries to have everything.'

'You know what bugs me?' said Mikki.

'What?' I said.

Mikki said, 'Remember Nick, that guy who worked with me in the Hot Pot? I never asked him for his address and phone number. Bummer, hey?'

I laughed when she said that. I was pleased because Bryan was over inside her, and for one of us at least, the way ahead was clear.

11

The next morning, Mikki and I got a letter from Bron. Rather than write out the same thing twice, Bron had sent Mikki the even-numbered pages and me the odd ones. The symbolism of that didn't go unnoticed.

Mikki and I had to get together to get the whole thing, but we couldn't agree who should read it first, so we took the pages Bron had sent us and read them out loud.

Dear You Two,

I really miss you. I wish I could be with you and talk to you because a lot of things have been happening. I hope writing some of them down is going to help me make sense of them.

When I arrived I felt incredibly nervous. I pushed my trolley out through immigration and when I saw all the people waiting at the barrier, my knees went to peanut butter. One guy really stood out because he was wearing this Hawaiian-shirt from Hell over a big paunch and he had grey hair that badly needed cutting and a fuzzy white beard that made him look like a cross between a hippie and one of the Seven Dwarfs. He was waving his arms around and going, 'Whoo!' I turned to see who he was waving at, and it was me. He was Dad. I thought, 'My God, he's turned into an American!'

Then we got close to one another and we both stopped. We were wondering what to do. We hadn't met for three years and we'd both changed. All the things that had happened to me that he hadn't been part of went zooming through my mind.

He said, 'You're so beautiful,' like he was really surprised.

I hugged him to put an end to the embarrassment of not knowing whether I ought to or not. When I hugged him, he didn't smell the same. He used to smell of board-markers and pipe tobacco, but now he just smells of deodorant.

We walked out to his car and he was asking me questions about the flight and my exams. I was dying to tell him that I knew all about him and Mum, and Steve being Ellie's real father, but every time a gap came up in the conversation it got filled with trivia. Then we got into the car and Dad said, 'I want to tell you about my partner.'

First I thought he meant a business partner, but when he said her name was Tessa and she was cooking supper, I realised he was telling me that 'partner' meant 'live-in lover'.

I was really annoyed that he hadn't told me about her before. One of the reasons I came here was to have a chance to be alone with him so we could really get to know one another. It was typical of Dad to put off telling me about Tessa until the last minute instead of being straight about it right from the start.

I tried to picture Tessa and I came up with the American female equivalent of Dad – middle-aged and overweight, with dyed hair, rhinestone-studded glasses and clothes about fifteen years too young for her.

Wrong again. Tessa is thirtyish, wholesome-looking and seven months pregnant. When she and Dad are together, you don't notice the age difference. In fact sometimes he acts so immaturely it's like Tessa is older than he is.

Dad's been lecturing at the university Summer School, so Tessa and I have had a lot of time to talk. It's interesting, Mum always talks about Dad as though he's a walking resentment, but Tessa talks about him as though he's a case-study. She's got a peculiar way of talking. She looks you straight in the eyes and talks without blinking. Every time she talks to me I notice that she's got fair eyelashes and I wonder why she doesn't use mascara.

Tessa uses lots of phrases like, 'being in touch with the mainspring of your potential'. They remind me of the slogans you see printed on those posters of frogs climbing up reeds or kittens clambering into tea-pots. When you first read them they sound really deep, but the more you think about them, the more you realise that they don't mean anything.

Tessa told me that when she met Dad he was in 'a downwardly-mobile, self-destructive, alcohol-abuse spiral' which means he was drinking heavily. I've always known that Dad had a drink problem because Mum took special care to make sure I knew, but when Tessa came into his life he'd almost drunk it all away.

She helped him to stop. I think he's put Tessa and

60

the baby into the place that drinking once had in his life. They talk about the baby all the time and they smile. They show so many of their teeth that I'm afraid when the poor little thing's born they're going to eat it.

Their obsession can be off-putting. They've got this book called, 'GROWING WONDER – YOUR PREGNANCY DAY-BY-DAY' and they use it like an Advent calendar. Every evening they read it to find out what stage of development the baby's at. It's illustrated in full colour with the kind of pictures I wouldn't advise looking at before you eat. In 'GROWING WONDER' labour is called 'birthing' and there's a chapter that's titled, 'The Father's Role in birthing'. This is Dad's favourite part of the book and he's very proud of himself for wanting to be there when the baby's born.

I said, 'Were you there when I was born?'

You should have seen the look on his face. He and Tessa smiled so hard you could hear their skin creaking. Dad said that sixteen years ago, Britain was a sexist society and men had been brainwashed into believing that their presence at the birthing wasn't necessary.

'That's a real shame,' said Tessa. 'Without the father there, the baby is born into an emotionally-deprived ambience.'

So, that's what's been wrong with me all these years! It's not because my hormones are haywire with adolescence, it's not because my parents messed up their marriage – it's because I was born into an emotionally-deprived ambience.

The moment Tessa said that, I realised that most of what she and Dad come out with is meaningless,

61

or crap, or both. The spooky thing is that they believe it means something.

I wish you were here with me. You could take them apart in about ten seconds. Wayne would shred them with jokes they wouldn't get and Mikki would tell them how much bullshit they talk. I have to be more tactful because they're feeding me, but there are times when I have to bite my tongue hard.

They're keen for me to stay on here. Dad says he can get me into an excellent school and Tessa says that helping her take care of the baby would give me 'a quality mothering-experience'. I'm not so sure that she doesn't mean she'd like an unpaid baby-sitter.

They've opted not to know the 'gender orientation' of the baby. If it's a girl, her name will be Jane and if it's a boy they're going to call him Anthony. I was relieved to hear that they hadn't chosen Californian-type names, like Star or Bough . . .

Look, all this sounds like I'm not having a good time, but I am. America is an exciting place, Dad can be really funny and Tessa is kind, but . . . I don't feel right. This is their home, not mine. I don't know if they've got room in their lives for a baby and me. To tell you the truth, I'm not sure I've got room in me for them. And I know this sounds arrogant, but if I stayed I might end up thinking the way that they do. More to the point, I might end up not thinking, the way that they do.

As soon as I read that part of the letter, I knew that Bron was feeling shut-out again. She was in the middle of another family group that seemed complete without her.

Bron thought of children as expressions of love – but after her mother and father split up, no one seemed to want to be reminded of the love that she was an expression of. It made Bron feel that she wasn't wanted either.

When we finished reading the letter, Mikki sighed and grinned a grin the size of a cat.

'Oh, good, she's having a bad time!' she said. 'That means she's coming back, doesn't it?'

'How should I know?' I said. I did know, of course, I just didn't want to give Mikki the satisfaction of being right.

12

I've stared at the calendar and I've rummaged in my memory until things are all over the place, but I can't pinpoint the exact date that Bron got back from America. It was either a Tuesday or a Wednesday, or maybe she flew in on Tuesday and we didn't see her until Wednesday.

It bothers me because I have a compulsion to know exactly where people were when, so I can look for hints and shapes and patterns. Perhaps it's my painter's mind looking for form; perhaps my mind just works that way and I was attracted to painting because of it.

Whichever day it was, Bron came back changed. Her eyes were loving, her hug was tight and her laugh still made the back of my neck tickle, but there was something different about her.

We took the same ramble we'd taken the evening before Bron left, as though we were trying to prove to ourselves that hello was as strong as goodbye. We talked about what had been happening: Mikki spoke about the Hot

Pot and Nick and Bryan; I talked about TC&W and my parents. Bron laughed, but she wasn't saying anything. She was observing Mikki and me – comparing what she remembered about us with the reality.

Mikki noticed it too, because out of nowhere she said, 'So how was America?'

Bron frowned, then smiled, then shrugged.

'All right,' she said. 'Tessa and the baby were a bit of a shock at first, but I got used to it, only . . . I missed you two and Ellie a lot . . . and Mum and Steve as well. I wasn't really expecting to miss them, but I did. Being with Dad and Tessa made me realise how honest Mum and Steve are. I belong here, with them.'

I said, 'Do they know?'

Bron said, 'We had a conference about it. Mum said she was relieved. Steve seemed really pleased. I feel like I can trust him more than I can trust my dad. Steve's more reliable.'

Belonging somewhere must mean letting yourself be owned by a place. People confuse it with fitting-in, but you can fit in by developing a thick skin and complete insincerity. Belonging must go deep inside you . . . or I presume that it must; personally, I've never felt it.

Accepting her mother's relationship with Steve made Bron accept things about herself. Other people had always seen Bron as intelligent, sensible and hard-working, and she'd been afraid of letting them down. Now she was beginning to see that they were right. She was happy about the future. I didn't think I could ever be happy until I'd discovered my real self. Back then, I still believed that there was a real self that *could* be discovered.

We all talked about being A level students – people who went to school because they actually wanted to be there. It felt strange and we got giggly about it.

'We can drink coffee in the Sixth Form Common Room!' said Mikki.

'We can sit at the front in assembly!' said Bron.

'We can use the Coke machine!' I said. 'God, it was worth all the agony of the exams, wasn't it?'

'Hey!' said Mikki. 'Remember how nervous I was before my Spanish orals?'

And the GCSEs discharged themselves. All the fears and hassles seemed ludicrous. I did an impersonation of the Exams Secretary taking a register, Mikki remembered some of the more scurrilous graffiti on the desks and Bron made fun of her fits of jitters.

Silliness is the most delicate part of any relationship – trust stays and emotions scar, but silliness evaporates almost as soon as it's there. While Mikki and Bron and I were laughing, I wondered whether the future was going to wither our friendship or develop it. Perhaps we'd always be meeting up together and laughing.

There was a slight diversion in the route of our walk, caused by a young couple on the corner of Ayer Road. They were in Deep Snog, totally oblivious to traffic, passers-by and the unromantic setting.

I said, 'They look like two sink-plungers stuck together, don't they?'

Bron said, 'Oh, aren't they sweet?'

Mikki said, 'Bloody hell – it's Suze!'

And so it was. Suzanne was locked in an embrace with Dave Allbright, so my advice to her about having nothing to do with boys had obviously done her a power of good.

I said, 'Should we break it up? I'm sure I could scrounge a crowbar from somewhere.'

Bron said, 'No, don't!'

Mikki said, 'Let's leave them alone and go the other way.'

We ducked down Montague Lane as quietly as thieves.

I was impressed by Mikki's tact.

'That was very sensitive of you,' I told her.

'Why spoil Suze's big moment?' she said. 'Anyway, I'll be able to blackmail her. I reckon threatening to tell Dad about it is worth at least a fortnight's peace and quiet.'

Laughter hasn't come so easily since then. Sometimes when I laugh at something, I feel guilty about it afterwards. I know it's completely irrational, but feelings are. Feelings keep us from becoming inhuman and intelligence keeps us from behaving like animals; and getting the right balance between the two is a real swine.

13

I went back to Northmeadows, just to look around. It was smaller than I remembered and it had that peculiar haunted feeling that empty schools have. I was looking for continuity, memories . . . myself, I suppose – but I wasn't there any more.

I didn't go back there entirely out of nostalgia but because of a sense of occasion. I was about to take a Significant Step in my life, entering the Sixth Form, and I'd taken Significant Steps at Northmeadows, too. Leaving the Infants for the Juniors, leaving the Juniors, then GCSEs, A levels, university were all important squares on the board-game of life, along with walking, talking and losing virginity. I've delayed going to university for a year. I'm going to bum round Europe and sort myself out, but the official name for it is taking a sabbatical. I seem to have taken a sabbatical about losing my virginity, too . . .

Induction Day arrived. Although it sounds as if it ought to have something to do with giving birth, it was actually a day of commitment because it was when Sixth Formers signed on to their courses.

When I went downstairs that morning, I found Mother and Father hovering expectantly round the breakfast table. There was a small package next to my plate.

'Well, Wayne!' said Father.

'Well, Wayne!' said Mother.

'Well,' I said, because it seemed to be the thing.

'So, off to join the Sixth Form,' said Father.

'Yes,' I said, 'but you will be seeing me again. It's not like the Foreign Legion.'

Father cleared his throat and his eyebrows danced as though they were engaged in a courtship display.

'Never had a Sixth Former in the family before,' he said. 'Your mother and I bought you a little something because – well, because . . .'

'Because we're proud of you,' said Mother.

Must I confess to a certain moistening of the eye? When it came to displays of affection, my parents were usually as spontaneous as a professional hit-man, so I was a little unprepared. Inside the box was a beautiful fountain-pen.

I didn't know what to say, and Father began to get antsy, as he always did in the presence of emotion.

'Good Lord!' he said. 'Look at the time! Must dash! See you this evening! All the best, Wayne!' and he left before I could say anything.

With the pen was a small piece of paper, on which Father had written a quote from William Blake.

'To see a World in a grain of sand
And Heaven in a wild flower.'

It was what he always wrote on special occasions – retirement cards, congratulations-on-the-new-baby cards and that sort of thing. I think it was the only bit of poetry he knew by heart, and I doubt if he actually understood what it meant, but it was nice of him to bother.

Mother said, 'It was his idea to buy you a present, you know.'

I said, 'Was it?'

I must have sounded surprised, because Mother said, 'Yes. He cares about you a great deal, Wayne, though he doesn't find it easy to show it. Your father can't help being the way he is any more than you can help being the way you are.'

This was something of a revelation: it meant that Mother was aware of my being a way I was. I suppose I should have talked to her about what she meant, but that might have lead to a deeper understanding, and I didn't need my parents to understand. I needed them to be a locked door that I could kick against until it flew open.

When I arrived at school, Mikki was on the front lawn under her favourite tree. The sunlight shone through the leaves and covered her with bright flecks. She saw me, got up and ran towards me. I braced myself to receive a speed-of-light kamikaze Mikki-hug.

And then the accident happened. When you see an accident, everything goes into slow-motion so you've got time to notice small details.

Mikki reaches the edge of the front lawn and she trips. Her eyes change first, they go from happy to apprehensive. Her arms spread out to try and keep balance and they make her look like an ungainly eagle. She falls forward, drifting like a leaf and her head goes smack into the midriff of an unfortunate passer-by. He had no idea that this was going to happen – nothing led him to expect a teenage girl in the solar plexus, and the look of shocked surprise on his face is a textbook classic. He grabs Mikki in a reflex movement and they tumble back against the safety railing that stands between the pavement and the teachers' car park.

By the time I reached them, time was running at normal speed again. Mikki was upright, but the young man she'd demolished was folded over like a pen-knife with a half-closed blade.

'Bloody hell fire!' he gasped.

'Sorry!' said Mikki.

'So am I!' said the young man.

Mikki said, 'Are you all right?'

'I'll live,' he said. 'It'll be agonising, but I'll manage somehow.'

He said it very well – his timing was almost professional – and Mikki cracked up laughing.

While she was cackling away, the young man straightened up and looked at her. I didn't know him. He had a longish face, mousy hair and pale eyes.

'Trust me to run across the local sadist,' he said.

'I'm not!' said Mikki. 'And you weren't run across, you were run into – there is a difference you know.'

'Either way it hurts,' said the young man.

Mikki lifted her nose haughtily – an expression she managed with surprising success – linked her arm through mine and we walked away.

'Who was that?' she whispered.

'No idea,' I said.

'My life in the Sixth Form is already a disaster and I haven't even signed up yet!' said Mikki.

As she said it, Bryan Eaves pulled up in his father's car and Katie Fairlight stepped out of it. She and Bryan were terribly kissy-kissy-miss-you-darling.

I said, 'Is *she* coming back to the Sixth Form? What's she going to study, make-up and massage technique?'

'Don't be such a bitch!' said Mikki.

I said, 'How much of a bitch would you like me to be?'

We met Bron and then we went into the hall to listen to a talk from the Head. We were feeling rather nervous, but the Head's speech quickly calmed us before going on to numb us completely. It was a longer version of the talk he'd given in the final Year Eleven assembly, which was itself a longer version of the talk he gave after the mock exams. Some of his audience had come to know it so well they could have joined in.

The Head had just tossed an unfunny joke on to the steaming pile of bumptious platitudes he was building, when someone behind leaned forward and whispered, 'Who's this guy?'

I turned and saw it was Mikki's collidee.

'The Head,' I said.

'Does he always chunter on like this, or is it a contest?' said the young man.

Mikki gave him a look that would have wilted a sequoia and said, 'You're new here, aren't you?'

'Aye,' he said.

'Well if you want to survive, shut up!' said Mikki.

That's when I knew that she liked him, though I don't think she knew it herself. I exchanged glances with Bron, and Bron smiled, and I knew that I was right.

14

The part of the Head's speech that everybody paid attention to was the end, because the silence that came afterwards sounded so great. We applauded respectfully, in recognition of the fact that being as boring as the Head took a special kind of talent.

After the speech came the really important part of the day – coffee in the Sixth Form Common Room. This was the place we'd eyed enviously on cold, rainy days when we'd peered in through the windows and seen Sixth Formers lounging about. Now it was our turn to be on the desirable side of the glass.

It wasn't as good as we'd imagined – but what is? The red-vinyl-leather-type chairs which had looked so luxurious from outside were shabby; grubby foam-viscera exuded through the tears. The walls were scratched and the doors of the wooden lockers looked as though they'd formed part of the defence system at Dunkirk.

'Lived-in, isn't it?' I said.

'Hmm!' said Bron.

'Je-sus!' said Mikki. 'What a bog-hole!' – an unpolished but accurate remark.

We bought some brown liquid that we were told was coffee and sat down on some gashed chairs to observe the rest of the Lower Sixth. The Lush Gang were languishing in a corner and I was just about to comment that whoever advised Ruth Critch to buy a short skirt had a cruel sense of humour, when the mousy young man appeared.

'Hello, there!' he said. 'Remember me? I'm the one who's new.'

I could feel spikes springing out over Mikki, but Bron smiled.

'Hello,' she said.

'I'm Jack,' said the young man. 'Mind if I sit down?'

'We don't mind if you turn cartwheels,' Mikki growled.

Jack took this as a yes – I couldn't make up my mind whether this meant he was brave, or incredibly stupid. He squealed a chair round so that we formed a straggling circle.

'I'm Wayne,' I said. 'This is Bron and this is Mikki. We're not new – we've been around a bit.'

'You speak for yourself,' said Mikki. She curled her top lip into a sneer that was so pronounced I think she might have been able to pick her nose with it.

Jack said, 'My family's just moved down here from up North.'

'What part?' said Mikki.

Near Huddersfield,' said Jack.

'Really?' said Mikki. 'I've got an aunt who lives in Huddersfield.'

'Oh,' said Jack. 'D'you know it, then?'

'Never been there,' said Mikki. 'Can't stand my aunt.'

Jack looked glazed for a second – people generally did after they'd been Mikkied for the first time – then he smiled as he realised that Mikki had set him up, and then an expression came over his face that made him look like a fish who's forgotten how to swallow.

'Are you all right?' said Bron.

'Oh – um – aye – yes!' said Jack.

'Anything wrong?' I said.

'Oh – well – I – er – no!' said Jack.

He was seeing Mikki and he was seeing in moonlight. Her face was pouring into him until he was in danger of overflowing.

Mikki stood up angrily.

'Come on,' she said to Bron and me.

'Where?' said Bron.

'Somewhere that's not here,' said Mikki.

We left Jack as stunned as a man with his head caught in an industrial press.

'You were a bit brutal with him, weren't you?' I said to Mikki when we got outside.

'He was only trying to be friendly,' said Bron. 'He's probably lonely.'

'That's not my problem,' said Mikki. 'I don't need that Yorkshire pudding coming on to me, thank you very much. Why doesn't he just sod off?'

'I'm sure he'd do anything to oblige a genteel young lady,' I said.

76

This was tap-dancing on the rim of an active volcano, but I couldn't resist it.

'Butt out, Wayne!' said Mikki. 'I'm not a young lady and I'm not genteel, all right? What you see is what you get.'

She'd turned her anger from Jack to me, where it wasn't going to do any harm.

Induction Day turned out not to be about (in the Head's words) the intellectual challenge of coming to terms with the in-depth study of specialist topics; it was about filling in forms and listening to teachers talking. At least it was all over by two-thirty.

After Mikki left us at the corner of Ryle Avenue, Bron and I walked part of our ways home together.

'Mum and Steve are getting married tomorrow,' Bron said.

She said it as though she'd thought about it until the thought was thoroughly washed, aired and ironed.

'How are you feeling?' I said.

Bron said, 'They're being really laid-back about it. They're going straight from the Registry Office to the supermarket.'

'How are you feeling?' I said again.

'All right,' she said. 'I'm glad for them. They were really pleased when I said I wanted to go to the ceremony.'

'It's nice to know that someone's happy,' I said.

'Are you and I and Mikki going to be happy?' said Bron.

'Now there's a question – and me without my crystal ball!' I said.

Bron smiled, 'Mikki's going to be happy, isn't she?'

'Yes,' I said.

As I said it, I remembered Mikki sitting in the shade of the cherry tree on the front lawn and I thought how much I wanted to make pictures that looked like that. It turned out to be impossible, because I confused the way I saw things with the way I felt about them.

You can't express feelings in pictures, you can only hide them.

There's a place on the island that I want to paint. I found it one afternoon when I went exploring. It's half-way up the mountain behind the apartment. The slope levels out into a sort of natural terrace. There are a few dove-grey boulders, one or two stunted olive trees and a strong smell of wild herbs and goats. All the plants that grow there are well-protected, with tough skins or terrifying spines. Everything is saying, 'Keep out. Go back.'

And then, at the side of the track, are the remains of a house, just a bit of wall and a pile of rubble. From the spot where the house stood there's a superb view out over the bay, but I don't want to paint the view – I want to paint the ruin.

Something failed there. Something broke so badly that it fell apart and wouldn't go back together – I can feel it. Someone built the house on the mountain, well away from everything else, and then dreamed and hoped. I like to imagine that on bad days the view from the front door gave them inspiration.

But it all went wrong. Whatever they were fighting won and the house fell down.

I think I could do a good painting of that place and hide all sorts of things in it. Not a painter of dreams, but a painter of where dreams used to be, that's me.

15

I wasn't invited to Bron's mother's wedding, of course, but for some reason I often dream about it. In the dream, the Registry Office is a cream building with white doors and window-sills. Bron is with Ellie in a patch of sunshine on the steps leading down from the porch. They're laughing. When Steve and her mother appear in the doorway, Bron shakes out a box of confetti. The confetti swirls around like tutti-frutti snowflakes, and it's Bron's resent-ment and fears and worries, scattered and twisting on the wind . . .

And then Mikki and I are there too. We walk up to Bron, and the three of us are astonished and happy to be back together.

I wish I could stop having that dream . . .

I don't know when it became traditional to spend the last Saturday night of the summer holidays at the Duke – probably when the landlord started serving alcohol to anyone who was tall enough to be visible above the bar – but everyone observed the tradition. I told Mikki I'd meet her there about eight. Bron didn't come because she was baby-sitting Ellie so that Steve and her mother could go out for a quiet meal together.

I walked to the Duke. The last part of the walk was down a narrow lane with no pavement. At the end of the lane stood a magnificent copper beech tree whose branches covered half the Duke's roof. It was an idyllic setting for a quaint little country pub, so it was a pity that the Duke was occupying the site.

I was just in the mood to be Wayne Taylor, Party Monster, but the mood turned out to be wasted because I miscalculated and arrived early. There wasn't enough clientele to muster a Conga. I bought myself a half – it was pointless getting drunk when there was nobody to share it with – and looked around for somewhere to sit, and there was Jack.

He was on his own and he looked awkward. I think he wasn't sure whether he knew me well enough to say hello or not, but I made up his mind for him. I walked over to his table and said, 'Anyone sitting here?' This was a stupid question since I could see that the other chairs were empty, but then politeness does involve a fair share of stupid questions.

Jack said, 'Help yourself,' and I did.

He was wearing a poorly-knitted grey sweater with a ragged hole in one wrist. I was very taken with it; it had a sort of in-your-face-sod-what-you-think style.

I was wondering what to say and covering the silence with a drink, when Jack said, 'Don't talk about the weather.'

I said, 'What?'

Jack said, 'It's a cliché, isn't it? When Brits start a conversation, they're always supposed to talk about the weather.'

'Or football,' I said.

Jack said, 'Don't talk about that, either. I can't understand football – except for the bits where they spit and kiss.'

I eyed the pint he was seated behind and said, 'How many of those have you had?'

'Just this,' said Jack. 'I'm poor, but I'm intense.'

'How did you find out about the Duke?' I said.

'Some guy told me it was a good place to meet people,' said Jack. He did a double-take around the semi-empty pub.

'Things will liven up a bit later,' I told him.

We talked. Talk is like a dance: you offer your hand in words and if a partner takes it you swing and sway together. One person leans forward and another sits back and they weave their hands about in time to the rhythm of speaking. There are set steps, but Jack didn't seem to know any of them. He'd come to the ball in rugby-boots – or perhaps he knew the steps so well he knew when it was more interesting to ignore them.

We made one another laugh and we made one another think a little, and then Mikki arrived. She saw Jack and was just about to get hostile when he stood up and held out his hand.

'Jack Tavener,' he said.

'Eh?' said Mikki.

Jack said, 'That's my name – Jack Tavener. Now you're supposed to tell me what your name is while we shake hands.'

'It's a bit formal, isn't it?' said Mikki.

Jack said, 'It's just an excuse to touch. Touching's nice. People are dead afraid of touching each other – have you noticed?'

And something remarkable happened, because instead of doing Jack Grievous Verbal Harm, Mikki shook hands with him. It would have been nice if the earth had shaken, or a bolt of lightning had struck them when their skins touched, but all that happened was that Mikki said, 'I'm Mikki Lutkin,' and Jack said, 'I know.'

Mikki said, 'Why have you got long nails on one hand and short nails on the other?'

'Because I play the guitar,' said Jack.

Mikki said, 'Oh. What sort of music do you like?'

And they were off.

When I was little, my parents took me on a trip to London Zoo. I found it a sad place: all the animals looked depressed, as though they understood that something was missing from their lives but they weren't certain of what it was. The only bright spot in the day was watching a pair of giant otters playing. They ran so close together they were almost entwined, and they rolled around in mock ambushes, pulling their snapping jaws back just short of biting.

Mikki and Jack were like that. Jack was

attracted to Mikki because he thought she looked beautiful, but he kept on discovering that there was far more to her than that. Mikki tried to be defensive, but she kept on forgetting and laughing at the things Jack said.

It might have been Bron who said that a good conversation should go nowhere and say everything, but it was probably me and it was probably being with Mikki and Jack that night that made me think of it. I didn't have much of a chance to join in their conversation, but watching it happen was fascinating.

By ten o'clock, any kind of talk was impossible. The Duke was packed with people singing along to the jukebox and misbehaving loudly.

'This place sucks!' said Mikki. 'Let's go outside for some air.'

'Must we?' I said. 'Passive smoking is so comforting.'

It was a warm September night, but it felt cool after the heat of the pub. The sky was clear and the moon was up and the big copper beech tree looked like a Rembrandt etching.

Jack said, 'I like the moon. One winter when I was a kid, I went for a drive across the moors with my dad. You couldn't tell what was snow and what was moonlight.'

I was watching Mikki as he talked. Something opened up in her face and then closed again so fast that I almost heard it snap.

'Underneath the moonlight, the world's still crap,' she said in her Ultra-Bitch voice. She

84

was being Tough Mikki, the girl who wasn't going to be taken in by soft talk.

I looked at Jack and he looked at me. There was a question-mark hanging over his head. Mikki wasn't a hard shell with a soft centre, she was hard and soft in totally unexpected places and getting to know her wasn't going to be easy for him.

I remember that later, after Mikki and I had got off the bus and were walking across the Green, I said, 'Jack's nice.'

Mikki said, 'Hmm.'

I said, 'You two seemed to get on very well.'

Mikki said, 'Hmm.'

I said, 'What are you going to say when he asks you out?'

Mikki said, 'What makes you think he's going to ask me out?'

There's nothing special about being a prophet – all you have to do is keep your mouth closed and your ears and eyes open.

16

Next morning, I bent the rules about New Place by phoning Bron and arranging to meet at her house beforehand. I wanted to tell her about Mikki and it wouldn't wait.

Bron's mother opened the door, and I hadn't gone very far down the hall before Ellie came running to head-butt me in the crotch.

'I'm big, Wayne,' she said.

I said, 'No, I'm Big Wayne, you're Little Ellie.'

Ellie said, 'You're silly.'

I said, 'All the interesting people are.'

Ellie said, 'I'm going to the Infants School tomorrow.'

I said, 'That makes me feel old.'

'Wait until you get to my age,' said Bron's mother.

'Yes,' I said. 'I may well have to.'

Bron was in the kitchen, helping Steve to wash up the lunch things. It was relaxed and cosy and it made a pang in me; I thought about the family I was never going to have and I missed it – a whimsical reaction, but painful nevertheless.

I didn't congratulate the newly-weds because I wasn't sure if I was supposed to know or not, but the house felt as though something important had happened.

Bron and I walked to New Place by a route we knew Mikki wouldn't take.

'Jack and Mikki have a thing going,' I said, 'but they don't know it yet.'

And I told her about what had happened at the Duke.

'I'm glad,' said Bron.

She was sad, too, because it wasn't happening to her. Mikki was ready for a new relationship and it had begun, but Bron was going to take a long time to find someone special. She wanted love to be like Ellie – totally trusting, unquestioning and spontaneous. I've always found that being spontaneous is best when you've worked out what you're going to say in advance.

Bron said, 'Do you daydream about relationships?'

I said, 'No,' which was true; I wouldn't have known what to daydream about. Whoever said that ignorance is bliss was really ignorant.

'I do,' said Bron. 'Sometimes it's silly and sometimes it's romantic.'

'And what would you like it to be in real life?' I said.

'Here,' said Bron. 'But not for a while yet. I think I need to get my future straightened out first.'

Bron had found out what she didn't want: she didn't want a relationship that would go wrong the way her parents had gone wrong; she didn't want to live in America – but she hadn't quite worked out what she did want. I don't think any of us had, and it didn't feel as though there was any particular rush. We thought there'd be time for everything. Parents and teachers kept telling us to slow down and be more patient – it was just youth making us feel that we had to hurry, and we believed them. They weren't wrong, but they weren't right either.

When Mikki arrived at New Place she looked grumpy. She was kicking along with her hands in her pockets and when she spoke it was obvious she was feeling newly-peeled and sensitive.

'The nerve of that guy last night!' she said.

Bron said, 'What guy?'

I said, 'Who, Jack?'

'Jerk is more like it,' said Mikki. 'He stuck to us like a leech all evening.'

'I thought he was charming,' I said.

'Well I thought he was smarmy,' said Mikki. 'Let's talk about something else.'

'You mentioned him first,' I said.

'So?' said Mikki. 'Have you got some kind of a problem with that? I mean, just because I happen to mention the guy doesn't mean anything, does it?'

'No!' I said.

'Of course not,' said Bron.

'Then why are you saying it like that?' said Mikki.

Bron said, 'Like what?'

Mikki said, 'Like it *does* mean something.'

Mikki didn't have mood-swings so much as mood-roundabouts that revolved so fast, everything was blurred together.

Bron changed the subject and talked about the wedding, I talked about A level courses, Mikki brooded and didn't say anything much.

I went home afterwards and did a drawing of Mikki. I drew her looking like a reflection in a pool of water. Ripples spread out from the middle of the pool, distorting the reflection until it was almost pulled into pieces. I was quite pleased with it.

Mikki rang me later.

'Guess what, Wayne?' she said. 'You'll never guess!'

I guessed at once, but Mikki would have been disappointed if I'd told her, so I said, 'Then you'd better tell me quick, before my Ovaltine goes cold.'

Mikki said, 'He rang me up and asked me out.'

'Who?' I said.

'Jack,' said Mikki.

'No!' I said. 'And what did you say?'

'Yes,' said Mikki.

She sounded embarrassed. He'd rung every Lutkin in the phone book until he found her, and as soon as he heard her voice, he asked her out. She'd been going to tell him to get stuffed, only somehow it had come out as 'yes'.

'D'you think I'm stupid?' said Mikki.

'No,' I said.

Mikki said, 'And you do think he's nice, don't you? I mean, really, really nice.'

I said, 'Mikki, if I thought he was any nicer I'd fancy him myself and you'd have a fight on your hands.'

Mikki said, 'Are you taking the piss?'

'Would I?' I said.

Mikki was at the paranoid stage, where every glance and every word has to be wrung dry of meaning. First you're pleased that someone's shown an interest in you, and then you get anxious about it – perhaps they feel sorry for you, or it's all some sort of twisted joke. I've been at that stage myself.

Unfortunately, I haven't been at any other stage.

17

Mikki told Bron and I all about her date with Jack the day after it happened. We went back to her house after school and sat in the kitchen, drinking coffee while Suzanne danced in her bedroom and made the ceiling thump.

Mikki described the date in so much detail – often jumping up out of her chair to act bits out – that I remember it in pictures, as though I'd actually been there with them. Some of what Mikki told us was in words and the rest was in the way she said them.

They were both nervous: Mikki twisted her arms together and laughed too loudly; Jack kept ducking down, as though apologising for his height. They met outside school, which was a place Jack could find without a map, and went walking. The talk was bitty at first, but ran more smoothly as they lost their nerves, and then they talked until the air was shadowy.

Mikki told Jack about Bryan. She hadn't planned it and she had no idea why she did it – talking about a past love on a first date is not recommended – but once the story started unwinding, she couldn't stop.

Jack listened without interrupting and when Mikki had finished, he told her about Lynne, his first love. It was a story about falling in love and being happy, and then being unhappy – like most love stories.

They were like patients in hospital, comparing scars.

Then a moth got tangled in Mikki's hair. Jack helped her to disentangle it and while this was happening they kissed. Mikki said it was because a kiss wanted to happen with her and Jack on either side of it.

As she told us, Mikki kept breaking off to ask questions:

'You know how it feels when you're going to kiss someone and it's like magnets are pulling you together?'

'You know when you're looking at someone and their eyes get bigger and bigger until you go right down inside them?'

I kept nodding and saying, 'Yes, I know,' but I didn't. I'd never felt those feelings, but I could get some idea of what they must be like from looking at Mikki. She glowed as she talked. There was a name for the glow, but no one mentioned it.

Bron and I were half-way up the front path when Suzanne came rushing out of the house. She ran up the path and grabbed my arm.

'You didn't say hello to me!' she said.

I smiled at her pretty pout and said, 'Hello. How are things with Dave?'

'I'm going out with Ben Curran now, but Dave still wants to go out with me. He keeps ringing me up,' said Suzanne.

'And who do you really like best?' I said.

'Matt Bailey,' said Suzanne. 'He hasn't asked me out yet, but I think he's going to.' Her eyes lost their mischief and went serious. She said, 'Wayne, am I your friend too? I mean, you don't just talk to me because I'm Mikki's sister, do you?'

I said, 'You don't need a friend, you need a guard.'

'Who do I need to be guarded from?' she said.

I said, 'You don't – other people need the protection.'

Bron and I walked up Mikki's street, thinking our own thoughts. I was wondering what Bron thought about it all, and what I thought about it all, and then Bron said, 'D'you think this is the beginning of the end?'

I said, 'Of what?'

'Of the Great Triangle,' said Bron. 'I mean, Mikki's going to want to be with Jack now, isn't she? Maybe she won't have time for us.'

'Perhaps not,' I said, 'but she'll know we're there if she needs us.'

'But what if it ends?' said Bron. 'What if we drift apart and never see each other again?'

Mikki and I had faced this question when Bron left for America – Bron had only just discovered it. We'd been so close for so long that the thought of not being close was frightening.

I said, 'We'll take what we learned from each other and we'll go off and live it.'

Bron thought about this for a while and so did I, because I was interested in working out what it meant.

Bron said, 'D'you like Jack?'

'Yes,' I said.

Bron said, 'Are you jealous?'

'Of whom?' I said. 'Jack, or Mikki?'

Bron said, 'I think I'm jealous of them both, of their togetherness.'

I said, 'Oh, togetherness isn't all it's cracked up to be.'

How would I have known? But I knew that togetherness was cracked up to be everything. It was in films, in songs, on TV; adverts tried to sell it, the news was full of stories about famous people and how they lacked it.

Bron suddenly said, 'Have you ever wondered about what might have happened if you and I had got together?'

I said, 'We are together.'

Bron said, 'I mean girlfriend-boyfriend getting together.'

'I've never thought about you that way,' I said. 'Or Mikki, either.'

Bron said, 'I know. It's never occurred to any of us. I wonder why not?'

'Because we're too interested in each other as people,' I said. 'Anyway, I don't want a complicated relationship with anyone. There are other things in life. I'd rather have a cup of tea and a digestive biscuit.'

And it was sad – but it was true.

18

A couple of days later I was in the Common Room at morning break when Bron came in looking as though she had news – and she did.

'I'm going to put my name forward in the Sixth Form Committee elections,' she said.

I said, 'Oh good. Will you do something about the coffee?'

Bron said, 'And I've joined the Debating Society and Drama Club.'

I made a face at this and Bron laughed. 'Look, if I'm going to be in the Sixth Form, I'm going to be in it right up to my neck,' she said. 'There's no point in not getting involved, is there?'

'Well, people leave you alone, for one thing,' I said.

Bron said, 'I don't want to be left alone.'

And she wasn't. She was elected on to the Sixth Form Committee and became indispensible; within a fortnight she was chairperson of the Debating Society and it wasn't long before Mr Coombs, Head of Drama, took to wandering into the Common Room and saying, 'Anyone seen Bronia Arnold around?'

I don't know if Bron got involved to try and make lots of new friends in case she lost her old ones, because I never asked her, but she certainly got herself noticed. Her entry into the Sixth Form Common Room was always accompanied by a communal sigh from any males who happened to be there.

I celebrated my entry into the Sixth Form by working. A lot of my fellow Sixth Formers seemed to have stayed on at school in order to strut about in designer casuals and get off with each other, but I studied hard. If I didn't do well, Father might think he was right and I knew that any conversation we had in which he told me so would be utterly intolerable. There are few things more repellant in life than a smug parent.

On the Friday of that week in September, something quite bizarre happened. At lunch-time, I was on my way to the Art Suite to collect a piece I'd finished the day before, when someone called my name; I turned around and it was Katie Fairlight.

The sun was on her hair, making it shine like spun platinum. She tilted her head on one side and blinked her blue dreamy eyes at me. She was trying to charm me into thinking she was all fluffy and feminine, but I wasn't fooled. I knew that beneath the bimbo-airhead mask lurked someone with the social skills of a Great White Shark.

Katie said, 'Wa-ayne?'

I said, 'Yes?'

She said, 'You're like really good mates with Mikki Lutkin, aren't you?'

I said, 'Yes.'

She said, 'Well, you know how Mikki like went to the Year Eleven Prom with my Bryan, right?'

I noticed the possessiveness in the possessive pronoun and said, 'Yes.'

Katie said, 'Well did anything like happen, sort of thing?'

I frowned. Katie had developed vagueness into a sort of art form and I wanted to be sure I understood what she was getting at.

'Happen?' I said.

'Yeah, you know,' said Katie. 'Did Mikki and Bryan get it together, sort of thing?'

There was something hard and sharp behind Katie's eyes. She had a tight hold on Bryan, and now she wanted to control his past as well. Mikki could do without Katie Fairlight on her back.

I said, 'Why don't you ask Bryan?'

I'd said the magic name. Katie went all coy and deepened her dimples.

'I did,' she said. 'He said they never done nothing. He said if she said they did, then she was jealous.'

'There you are then,' I said. 'You know how much you can trust Bryan.'

Katie had a genuine flair for malice, but she didn't understand irony at all and she tottered away happy. I breathed a sigh of relief that I'd been able to protect Mikki from her and understood how knights felt just after they'd slain dragons.

In New Place on Sunday, Mikki talked so much about Jack that Bron and I made fun of her.

'Leave it out!' said Mikki. 'Just because I'm happy for a change!'

'Really?' I said. 'That wouldn't have anything to do with super mega-wonderful Jack, would it?'

Mikki said, 'Look, I know you're probably going to think that I'm a right tart, but I – I mean Jack and I have, sort of . . .'

'Are you trying to tell us that you and Jack have expressed your feelings for one another by physical means?' I said.

'Yes,' said Mikki, 'and he was sweet, and gentle, and considerate and—'

'Don't go on, or I shall be forced to hurl,' I said.

Mikki was as happy as fireworks that afternoon, and the sparks spread into Bron and me and we laughed a lot.

'I feel great,' said Mikki. 'I want you two to feel great as well.'

'Are you going to bring him here?' said Bron.

Mikki put herself on hold for a long time while she thought about it.

Eventually she said, 'No. This is the three of us. Jack and I can find special places of our own.'

She was already thinking of the future in terms of Jack, as though she sensed that it was going to last.

I said, 'If we cut New Place into three pieces and we each carried a piece, if we ever split up we'd be able to recognise each other when we were old by fitting the pieces back together.'

Bron said, 'We already do carry pieces around.'

Mikki said, 'We're never going to split up.'

I said, 'If anything happens to me, I want you to share my bit of New Place between you.'

Mikki said, 'Nothing's going to happen to you.'

Bron said, 'You never know what's going to happen.'

Mikki was sure about her feelings, Bron had learned that feelings can lead to unsureness, I was unsure of what feelings might lead to.

We said other things and laughed at them, but I don't remember what they were. I didn't pay particular attention – it was just another time in New Place.

Memory is like a kaleidoscope. It's made up of the same pieces, but each time you hold it up and look through it, it's different. Things that once made you ashamed make you laugh out loud when you look back on them; things that were painful just make you smile; but ordinary things, things you didn't really notice at the time, can make you weep, because ordinary things make up most of our lives.

19

One day that week I went with Bron to meet Ellie from Northmeadows. The kids erupted out through the doors and then formed lumps, like cooling lava.

Bron said, 'It's all happening too quickly. One minute you're running out of Infants school and then before you know it you're waiting for your own children.'

I said, 'You've still got some time to go before then.'

'Mikki wants her children to spend half the year with me and the other half with you,' said Bron. 'She says it's the only way she can be sure of getting on with them.'

I said, 'Children shouldn't get on too well with their parents – they turn out normal because they've had happy childhoods. I'd rather loathe my parents and be a star.'

Bron said, 'I had a long talk with Jack the other day.'

I said, 'Oh?'

Bron said, 'You're right. He is nice. Have you noticed his eyes?'

I said, 'Yes. They're just above his nose, aren't they?'

That wasn't what Bron had meant and I knew it – and what she did mean concerned me vaguely, though I don't know if *she* knew what she meant.

This must have happened on Wednesday, because my parents' wedding anniversary was the day before and I was still feeling annoyed by Father's reaction to my present.

I'd painted them a picture. It was an oil painting of two dark blue oblongs on a pale grey background. Between the oblongs was a pink circle. I'd taken care with it so that the paint looked smooth on the canvas. When she saw it, Mother made a noise like knitting-needles clacking together and father cleared his throat.

'That's what you'd call Modern Art, is it?' he said.

I said, 'Yes. I only finished it yesterday and you can't get much more modern than that.'

Father smiled and said, 'The blue bits are your mother and I and the pink blob is you, I suppose?'

I was really irritated by this comment because Father was right, but I wasn't going to give him the satisfaction of knowing that he was right.

I said, 'Yes. We're on the beach at Margate.'

Father said, 'But we've never been to Margate.'

'It was a joke,' I said.

'Why?' said Father. 'Is Margate funny?'

I let it drop; winding him up had lost all its savour.

Father made a fuss about hanging the picture at once and he went to find a hammer and a picture hook in the cupboard under the stairs. While he was out of the room, Mother said, 'Do you think you might change one day, Wayne?'

She approached me with cautious prods, like a dish she'd never eaten before.

'In what way?' I said.

Mother said, 'One goes through all kinds of phases as one grows up. It can be quite a perplexing time.'

I thought – Tell me about it! – and then I realised that Mother wasn't only talking about my wanting to be a painter.

Mother said, 'You can always talk to me about it if—' She broke off because Father came back into the room and the atmosphere changed. I was relieved. The idea of Mother as a confidante was a little too much for me to handle. I never took her up on her offer, because there are things it's absolutely impossible to discuss with your parents – like their sex-life and anything that's really important to you.

I didn't talk to Mother, but I did talk to Jack. It was during a private study session on Thursday morning. I was in the school library, brushing up my Post-Impressionists, when Jack appeared and started talking to me.

I said, 'Tell me, Jack, does your old grey sweater really smell of teddy-bears?'

Jack laughed and said, 'Mikki told you! Does she tell you everything?'

'Just edited highlights,' I said. 'Though she does do slow-motion replays. Does she tell you everything?'

'She says you're a bloody good mate,' said Jack.

'Then that's everything,' I said. 'Have you met Mikki's sister yet?'

'No,' said Jack.

I warned him what to expect. It was only fair: Suzanne wasn't exploring her sexuality so much as colonising and exploiting it and she was likely to come at Jack like a high tide.

I think Jack had made up his mind to get on with Mikki's friends. It didn't take long with me, because I liked him and as we talked I got the feeling that he liked me. I wasn't used to this, as most males of my age approached me with a morbid curiosity and had conversations composed almost entirely of unasked questions.

'Are you and Mikki serious?' I asked.

'Are you asking me if my intentions are honourable?' said Jack.

'Yes,' I said.

Jack laughed because he thought I was joking, and I laughed because he thought I was joking, and when he was good and relaxed, I talked about something that was bugging me.

'So,' I said. 'You've been talking to Bron?'

He laughed and shook his head.

'Does anything get past you?' he said.

I said, 'No.'

And nothing did, not even the little flash of guilt that came into Jack's eyes.

'Did Mikki tell you about that as well?' said Jack.

'No,' I said. 'Bron did.'

And then Jack did something that totally disarmed me. He was honest. He said, 'Bron's really nice, you know. I think if I'd met her first instead of Mikki . . .'

'But you didn't,' I said.

'No, I didn't,' said Jack. 'So there it is.'

Just for a moment I thought it might be possible. I pictured Jack at New Place with Mikki, Bron and me, the Great Triangle transformed into the Great Parallelogram – then I remembered that he and Mikki were seeing in moonlight. It was roses, not carnations. Sex may be liberating, but it brings a lot of problems along with it; it's like opening Pandora's Box, only without the Hope.

Friday lunchtime, Jack and Mikki and Bron and I sat about in the Common Room eating egg rolls.

Jack said, 'Are we all meeting at the Duke tonight, then?'

Mikki said, 'How many times do I have to tell you? It's *up* the Duke, *down* the supermarket, *over* the newsagents'.'

'You and your fancy Southern ways!' said Jack.

'I can't,' said Bron. 'I've got an improvisation workshop with a bunch of Year Nine kids tonight.'

'How about you, Wayne?' said Mikki.

I made some excuse, but the truth was that I didn't want to feel in the way.

'Be a miserable old sod, then!' said Mikki. 'While we're having a brilliant time, we won't think of you at all.'

Bron was looking worried.

I said, 'What's wrong?'

She said, 'There's a dodgy fader on the lighting-board in the Drama Suite. I meant to tell Mr Coombs about it but he's off ill.'

'And?' I said.

'And it might be dangerous,' said Bron. 'I don't want some Year Nine kid mucking about and having an accident with it.'

'Simple,' I said. 'Kill anyone who goes near the lighting box and then no one will get hurt.'

I spent the evening listening to music and reading my book of Japanese poetry, thinking that I might do illustrations for it as part of my Design coursework.

The rest of my memory is quite clear. I took off my headphones and heard the music for the end of News at Ten coming from the television downstairs. I fancied a cup of coffee and I went to make one. Mother and Father were getting ready to go to bed and I asked them to leave the television on because there was a comedy show on Channel Four that I wanted to watch.

It wasn't a very funny edition of the show, but I watched it all the way through. It was followed by one of those chat-shows that get you hooked because you keep wondering when something interesting is going to happen.

A musclebound Hollywood-actor's mother was being interviewed about what it was like having a musclebound Hollywood-actor as a son. The interview wasn't going very well because the American woman couldn't understand the interviewer – partly because of his peculiar accent and partly because he was a complete cretin.

The phone rang. I looked at my watch and it was late. I wondered who it could be. I picked up the phone and a voice said, 'Can I speak to Wayne, please?'

I said, 'Speaking.'

The voice said, 'I'm afraid I've got some terrible news for you, Wayne. Mikki was knocked over and killed tonight on her way home from the pub.'

20

In films, when people hear tragic news they scream, or put their hands to their mouths and say, 'Oh, my God!'; in Victorian novels they faint.

I didn't.

I said, 'What?' and when the voice came again and told me Mikki had been killed and then gave me the details, I said, 'Oh.'

I thought – Is this a phone? Is this real? Is this me?

I found out later that it was Mikki's mother who had called me. I didn't recognise her voice at the time, but then I was having trouble recognising myself.

When I put the phone down, I didn't feel anything. I remember thinking that I was supposed to be crying, but I didn't have any tears. I went to make myself another cup of coffee. I didn't want one, I just felt as though I ought to be doing something.

I took the coffee into the lounge, turned off the television, turned off the lights, drew back the curtains and stared out of the window. I kept telling myself – Mikki's dead. She's been killed. It wouldn't go in. There was a sheet of plate-glass between me and everything else and the truth kept bouncing off it. I kept expecting someone to ring and tell me it had all been a mistake, or a sick joke, but the call didn't come and I fell asleep in the armchair in the early hours of Saturday morning. I didn't dream, and when I woke up it was all still there . . .

Mikki left the pub with Jack at ten-thirty. They turned down the offer of a lift – they must have had lots to talk about and they wanted to stretch out the time together. At ten thirty-five they passed the bus-stop just as a bus pulled up. Tony Birch shouted to them, asking them if they were going to get on or not. They laughed and waved.

At ten forty-five a passing car went out of control, mounted the pavement and knocked them both down. Jack had head injuries and his right leg was broken; Mikki was killed instantly.

People say that when someone close to you dies unexpectedly, first you're glad it wasn't you and then you feel guilty. I wasn't guilty or sad – I was nothing. My mind was like a half-crushed insect, trying to carry on as though the damage hadn't happened. I kept coming up against the brick wall of Mikki's death and there was no way over it, or round, or under. I couldn't think it away, or paint it away and talking wouldn't make it disappear.

By mid-afternoon on Saturday I was starting

to panic. I knew that sooner or later the huge emptiness inside me was going to fill up with something and I wasn't sure that I could cope. I needed to see Bron and I actually got as far as the front door before I realised that seeing Bron again was one of the things I was afraid of. What was I going to say to her? What could be said?

This was the start of a storm of questions that went howling through me.

Why Mikki? Why did she have to be dead when so many crap people were still walking around? Why couldn't it have happened to one of them? Why hadn't she accepted the lift – or caught the bus? What if I'd gone to the Duke? Would she have left a few seconds earlier, or later? What was the last thing she said? What was the last thing she saw? Did she know the car was going to hit her and was she terrified?

I had to find the place where it happened. I wanted reasons, I wanted to blame someone or something. I couldn't blame the driver of the car because people don't mean to have accidents. I couldn't blame God because I was a failed agnostic. For years I'd tried to believe that I was uncertain about whether God existed or not, but deep down inside I had faith that He wasn't there, or I would have shaken my fist at the sky and raved.

It was easy to find. I thought somebody had been selling flowers at the side of the road and abandoned the stall, but the flowers were all for Mikki – bunch after bunch of them, carrying cards with messages I couldn't bear to read, though I spotted a lot of names I recognised.

I looked around, wanting to fix the place in my mind. It was an ordinary place to be significant: next to a hedge, just past a speed-limit sign. Mikki and Jack had been walking on the left, so the car had come up behind them. She couldn't have known a thing about it.

Have you ever tried not to think about something? People say, 'Don't think about it. Just think about something else,' as though it were easy. I didn't want to think about the accident, but as I walked back I couldn't stop myself. I thought about the sweep of the car headlights, and the bang of the impact, the jangling of broken glass over and over again. I added variations – Mikki shouting, Mikki laughing just before it happened – until I wanted to split my head open so that all the thoughts would spill out.

Just past the 'PLEASE DRIVE CAREFULLY THROUGH OUR TOWN' sign I saw something lying in the gutter. It was a bird that had been hit by a car. I didn't recognise it as a bird at first. It was almost impossible to think that tiny scrap of feathers had once been alive. I saw the way the car had broken its fragility, and that's when I cried about Mikki for the first time.

I lay awake that night and whispered into the dark. I said, 'I hadn't finished talking to you. There was more to say. There were things

I wanted to tell you about and show you. I wanted to find out about what you'd find out. I wanted to share . . .'

It didn't help; nor did thinking about unlaughed laughs and unhugged hugs and all the pointless, colourless misery of everything.

21

I must have told my parents and I suppose they were sympathetic but I don't remember the form their sympathy took. I have a vague recollection of Father mumbling something about a waste of a young life and that's all.

I remember the coincidences, though. They started almost straight away. When I got in, the radio was on in the kitchen and there was a news item about fatal accidents on the road being fewer than at any time since the war. That night a popular hospital series screened an episode that was all about a motorway pile-up. One of the Sunday newspapers had a report about a mother who claimed to be in touch with the spirit of her teenage daughter who'd been knocked over and killed. One of the actresses in a film that was shown on Sunday afternoon was called Kim Lutkin . . . the coincidences went on and on until I was convinced that there was a conspiracy to keep on reminding me.

On Sunday evening I went to see Mikki's family. It's difficult to explain the atmosphere in the house, but it wasn't anything like I expected. It was like a party mixed with a group-therapy session. Various people Mikki had been friendly with were seated in groups on the floor of the lounge. They were talking about Mikki and drinking lager that was supplied by Mikki's parents.

Mikki's parents seemed almost shockingly cheerful, but above their smiles they had the eyes of refugees or famine victims. I think they were being strong for Mikki's friends because most of us were dealing with grief for the first time.

Suzanne gave me a hug and I could feel that her shoulders were trembling. Inside the hug I said, 'How are you?'

'I'm all right,' she said. 'How are you?'

'Not too good,' I said.

Suzanne kept her arms around me but leaned back so that she could see my face.

'We're worried about Bron,' she said. 'She came over yesterday and spent the night in Mikki's room. She hasn't spoken yet.'

'Where is she?' I said.

Bron was in the kitchen, seated at the table where we'd sat when Mikki told us about her date with Jack.

She looked like something cast up on a beach. Her eyes were glassy, her hair was lank, and she didn't just have a blank face – her whole body was vacant.

It must have been about two metres from the doorway to her chair, but it was one of the longest walks I've ever taken. I had to cross years as well as distance, and memories of the Great Triangle were going off in my brain like flash-bulbs at a press conference.

I put my hands on Bron's shoulders. She stood up, turned and clung to me like one of those koala toys that cling to your pencil. I felt a wave of something that took me to a place where language hadn't been invented and things swirled around like the rainbows on the surface of a soap-bubble.

Words didn't happen until later, when Mikki's dad suggested that I take Bron out for a walk. She walked with her head resting on my shoulder, the way she had on the night before she left to go to the States.

I said, 'I've been trying to think of something to say for the last two hours, and this is the best I can come up with.'

Bron didn't say anything. I wasn't even sure if she knew who I was.

I said, 'It just doesn't make sense. She's going to walk round the next corner, isn't she?'

Very quietly, Bron said, 'I can't—'

I said, 'I know. Neither can I.'

Bron said, 'It's not right.'

It wasn't. People you love shouldn't have accidents; children shouldn't die before their parents; friendships shouldn't be broken until all the sharing has been used-up.

Bron said, 'It hurts.'

'It only lasts forever,' I said.

Bron said, 'Why do people I love always go away?'

114

I said, 'I'm not going away . . .'

But it wasn't going to be the same, and we both knew it. We were broken china, and even if we managed to glue ourselves back together, we were always going to be able to see the cracks.

Two years on, I can still taste the despair . . .

Mikki's funeral wasn't about death, it was a celebration of Mikki's life. There was no religious service – Mikki wouldn't have wanted one – and Mikki's parents said that people should wear whatever felt appropriate. I wore my silk jacket and a tomato-soup coloured shirt with my black jeans and Bron wore a long, white dress.

Mikki's mother and father made a speech – some of it made people laugh and some of it made them cry. I don't know how Mikki's parents did what they did, but it changed the way I thought about courage. When the speech was over, two of Mikki's favourite songs were played and then we all filed out into the sunshine.

One of the first people Bron and I met outside was Bryan. I felt Bron's arm tighten round my waist.

Bryan said, 'That's the way funerals ought to be.'

I said, 'It's a shame it wasn't somebody else's.'

Bryan gave me a fake smile, and then his face went all solicitous as he looked at Bron. 'How are you taking it?' he said.

Bron said, 'Piss off, Bryan.'

His face was like a stained-glass window and his thoughts shone straight through. You could see him not understanding why Bron was so hostile, and then you could see that he did understand. He said, 'I, er, only wanted to—'

Bron said, 'Take what you want and stuff it, Bryan.'

She might have said something else, but then Suzanne appeared and crept in under my left arm. Bryan turned around and walked away.

'Mum and Dad and I went to see Jack yesterday,' Suzanne said. 'He's going to be all right, but he doesn't remember anything about the accident.' She turned to me and there was a brightness in her face and a darkness behind it. 'He doesn't know Mikki's dead yet,' she said. 'When we left, he asked us to give her his love. Dad says he's going to need a lot of help getting over it when he finds out.'

Mikki's family had become very concerned about Jack. I think it was important to them that he recovered, because it would mean something good had come out of the accident.

I would rather have helped Mikki to get over Jack's death, but I didn't say so because it would have sounded too unkind.

Suzanne could tell I was thinking something depressing and she tried to make me more positive.

'Loads of people came, didn't they?' she said.

116

I said, 'Lots of people loved Mikki.'

When I said it, Suze's face went serious.

'You've still got me, Wayne,' she said.

After the funeral, there was a party at Mikki's house, but Bron and I didn't go there straight away. We slipped off to New Place.

Since Mikki's death, I'd been doing a lot of last times, thinking – The last time I wore this shirt, Mikki was alive; the last time I used this sketch-pad was the morning of the accident.

New Place was the biggest last time of them all.

Bron and I held hands as we walked down the path towards the stile, like Hansel and Gretel walking through the forest.

Bron said, 'We're lucky.'

I said, 'Oh?'

Bron said, 'Mikki only had a short life. We were really lucky to be a part of it, and have her as part of our lives.'

The idea helped her all the way to the stile, then she shook her head and said, 'I can't do it, Wayne.'

I said, 'We have to.'

Bron said, 'But if she isn't in New Place, she isn't anywhere!'

I said, 'Bron, we've got to let her go.'

And we did. We crossed the stile into New Place, and Mikki wasn't there, and Bron and I cried because we were.

When we were cried-out Bron said, 'Let's not come here any more. It's too sad now.'

I said, 'Yes, you're right,' because the only other words I could think of were clichés – life goes on, you can't live yesterday over again . . .

As we were leaving, it occurred to me that in the past other people might have used New Place the way that we had. That got me wondering about the people who were going to discover it in the future. It was as if we'd had our time at New Place and now it was someone else's turn. I took a last look back over the stile and hoped whoever found it would take good care of it, and each other.

22

When people talked about Mikki, they kept on saying, 'What a waste.' This irritated me, because it was as though they were saying that the life Mikki had missed was more important than the life she'd had. I couldn't think that. Mikki made me feel that I was lovable and knowing her had changed my life so totally that she was a large part of me. How could her life have been a waste when she was me?

The Monday after the funeral, Bron and I walked to school together. We kept reminding one another of places where Mikki's memory was going to be strongest because we didn't want to come across them unexpectedly.

Bron said, 'Our form room last year.'

I said, 'The Sixth Form Common Room.'

Then we both said, 'The tree!' and we laughed.

We laughed because Mikki's tree was on the school's front lawn and she used to sit under it when she was in a bad mood about something.

'Oh, God, I'm laughing!' said Bron. 'People will think I don't care.'

'People can get stuffed,' I said.

Bron bit her bottom lip and took a juddering breath.

'I wish I could talk to her about it,' she said. 'If I could pick up a phone and talk to her – just for five minutes – I think it would make it better.'

I said, 'I've got Mikki-shaped empty space right in the middle of me and everything else is just stuck round the outside of it.'

Bron said, 'You know how, when you're in love, the person you're in love with is the last thing you think about before you go to sleep and the first thing you think about when you wake up?'

'Hmm,' I said.

'That's how I am about Mikki,' said Bron. 'I didn't know grief was so much like love.'

'And I didn't know love was so much like grief, but I'll bear it in mind,' I said.

Going to school meant going back to work, and I did. At the time I thought I knew what for, but when I remember it now, it's as though I was in a fog. Most of the paintings and drawings I did that autumn make me shudder now: everything's on the surface, bright, cheerful colours and fussy details. There's a picture of the Art room that's almost frightening, because it makes the place look as thin as an eggshell that's about to crack and show the nothingness inside it.

I took to visiting the Duke twice a week,

hanging round the outer fringes of the Lush Gang and making them laugh with a few bitchy cracks. I found out how to get drunk and I also found out that there was nothing in it except more of what I was trying to get away from. At the time, I thought I was throwing myself into my life, enjoying myself to the full, living every moment as though it were my last, burning my youth with a bright flame and lots of other tinselly clichés. I thought I was being self-destructive and Romantic.

Actually, I was behaving like a plonker.

Bron and I weren't exactly avoiding one another, but we didn't have that much contact. Her school productions, debates and Sixth Form Committee meetings took up a lot of her time inside and outside school and it always seemed that we were both too busy for a real talk. We met in the Common Room and around the school, but that was just chatting. We stopped really talking because we knew that if we really talked it would be about Mikki and that it would make us upset, and getting upset would be a bad thing to happen.

I'd always thought that after people died you cried for a bit, then you stopped crying and that was it. I thought you missed them in some vague way, thought of them kindly on their birthdays and at Christmas and carried on as normal. I hadn't realised that it would be like a disabling illness and that I wouldn't be able to carry on as normal, because 'normal' had changed.

I thought I was coping fine until my Art

teacher, Mr Trevor, asked me to come and see him for a chat after school. When I got to his room, I found Mr Trevor looking at some of my paintings. They were spread out on the big table in front of him and he was leafing through them. I was used to having my efforts praised and I steeled myself to be gracious.

Mr Trevor said, 'It's not happening, is it, Wayne?'

I said, 'Sorry?'

Mr Trevor said, 'Your work. It's . . .'

'A-grade standard?' I said. 'You've been giving me As.'

Mr Trevor said, 'Yes, if you carry on churning out work like this, you'll get an A at A-level, but . . .'

'Sorry, Mr Trevor,' I said, 'I just wanted to see if I've got this straight – the work I'm doing is going to get me an A at A-level and there's a *but*?'

'The work's not going anywhere,' said Mr Trevor. 'I was hoping for something a bit more interesting from you. This is stuff done by a clever A-level student, not by a painter.'

Mr Trevor had really hit me where I lived and I blushed.

'You used to put yourself into your painting,' said Mr Trevor. 'Now you're holding it all back and putting in technique instead. I don't know what's going wrong, but . . .'

Another but. I don't think Mr Trevor knew what the end of the sentence was, but he'd told me straight and I was blushing because he was right.

I walked out of the Art room and stood in the corridor, looking at the view over the school buildings. I knew I wasn't putting myself into my Art work, because I'd deliberately lost me. Finding me again would mean facing up to life without Mikki, instead of running away from it to the Duke with the Lush Gang. If I didn't find myself again soon, I'd spend the rest of my life not facing things.

And right then, when I most needed to know that Mikki wasn't there, she was there. I heard her voice in my head.

'Wayne,' said Mikki's voice, 'if you screw up because of what happened to me, I'll bloody kill you!'

So I went straight home and I drew her every way I could think of and every way I could remember her. A lot of paper ended up in the bin, but each time I scrapped a drawing, I learned something.

I ended up with a picture of Mikki dancing. A number of lines flow across the paper and come together in the middle to make the rough outline of a person. The lines are Mikki's energy, and her words, and the movements of her arms and legs, and my remembering how beautiful she was. When the drawing was finished I knew it was all right to go on being upset.

23

Next morning I called for Bron on the way to school, which I hadn't done for ages. While I was waiting for her in the lounge, Ellie fastened on to me.

'Have you come to take me to school?' she said.

I said, 'No, I'm going to school with Bron.'

Ellie said, 'Bron's old enough to go to school by herself.'

'I know,' I said, 'but I'm not.'

Bron appeared and peeled Ellie off me. Ellie went rushing out of the lounge to find Steve.

Bron said, 'Want to talk?'

I said, 'Yes.'

Bron said, 'Something wrong?'

I said, 'Yes.'

Walking along the road, we fell into a silence. It wasn't the old, comfortable silence – it was something spiky and awkward and neither of us knew how to break it.

I said, 'I miss her laugh.'

I hadn't known I was going to say it, but once it was said it seemed a logical place to start. Bron was so surprised that she almost asked me who I meant, but then she realised that she knew and her silence deepened.

I said, 'I miss her being outrageous. I miss her being angry. What do you miss?'

Bron said, 'Please, Wayne, let's not talk about her. It'll only make us sad. She wouldn't have wanted us to be sad.'

I said, 'And you think pretending that nothing happened is going to make us happy?'

Bron stopped walking. She looked at me and her eyes were hurt.

'I'm not pretending that nothing happened!' she said. 'How can you say that?'

I said, 'Because not saying things isn't any good. It's like we're holding on to our own private bit of grief because it's all we've got left of her. I think we ought to give it away to one another.'

Bron thought about it for a moment and said, 'All right.'

We started to walk again.

I said, 'Mikki was so good at getting angry about things that I used to let her do my anger for me. Now I'm going to have to get angry for myself and I don't know if I can do it.'

Bron said, 'I didn't know somebody like Mikki could die. Old people die, or people who are really ill, but not Mikki. It scares me.'

'Everyone's frightened of dying,' I said.

I said it because I knew it was what people said when other people mentioned death. It was only when I said it to Bron that I realised how stupid it was. Knowing everybody else is as frightened as you are isn't much comfort, is it?

Bron said, 'It's not dying that frightens me, it's living. You never know when it's going to come to an end. There might be so little time to make sense of things.'

I said, 'Life doesn't make sense, it just happens.'

We'd believed too many poems about the journey of life and the voyage of life. The poems had made us think of time as being a wide road or an ocean. Mikki's death had made us understand that time is a needlepoint of now, always moving and gone the moment it's there.

That walk to school made Bron and I open up to one another again. She told me that Jack was home from hospital and that she'd been visiting him. I wasn't very easy with this idea, but I didn't say anything about it then. I could tell that Bron thought she was helping him, and Bron was only really happy when she had someone to help.

Jack returned to school at the end of November. He walked with a stick and he had a scar across the bridge of his nose but otherwise he looked much the same. I don't know why it should have surprised me, but it did. I suppose I'd expected something more dramatic, like his hair having turned white from shock.

One morning in the Common Room, Jack and I had our inevitable conversation about the accident. He frowned as he was talking and shifted in his chair, as though his leg was paining him.

'It's weird,' he said. 'I remember taking Mikki to the pub, and then there's nothing. It's like, I open the pub door and wake up in a hospital bed.'

Jack's shifting turned to squirming. Part of him remembered what had happened, but it wouldn't let the rest of him know.

I was disappointed. I wanted to know everything Mikki had said and done that evening – what she'd drunk, what music she'd listened to, what jokes had made her laugh. Jack sensed my disappointment and squeezed my arm.

'Sorry, Wayne,' he said.

'Not to worry,' I said. 'That's an awful walking stick you've got there, by the way.'

'What's wrong with it?' said Jack, holding the stick up to look at it. 'Grey steel looks very practical.'

'That stick doesn't look practical, it looks brutal!' I said.

Jack said, 'It's to help me with my limp.'

'Your limp what?' I said.

We resorted to stupid jokes for a while. It was a safer sort of conversation, all brightly lit by smut and with no shadowy corners – and then suddenly Jack looked over my shoulder and smiled at someone. He put so much of himself into the smile that I turned to see who it was; and it was Bron.

'You two look like a pair of old men gossiping on a park bench,' she said.

'And you look terrific!' said Jack, trying to turn it into a joke and not quite succeeding.

Bron sat down next to me.

'Have you told him?' she said to Jack.

'No. I was just going to,' Jack said.

I said, 'Told me what?'

Bron said, 'Jack and I are going to the Duke on Saturday night. You will come with us, won't you?'

I said yes, but I don't think Jack was too happy. I knew he was going to the Duke to lay Mikki's ghost and I knew he'd want moral support, but I wondered if it was *my* moral support he wanted. I didn't think he was playing up to get Bron's sympathy, but I didn't think he'd shy away from the chance to be comforted by her.

When we got to the Duke on Saturday evening, Jack had to hold Bron's hand to cover the fact that his was shaking, and he looked pale, but after a few minutes it was just a pub. We got drunk very quickly on very little, and we talked a lot about nothing in particular. We laughed a lot. The more feeble the joke the louder we laughed; people must have thought we were on speed.

You know the old saying *I didn't know whether to laugh or cry*? Well sometimes there's absolutely no difference between tears and laughter.

24

Bron and Jack were often together in the days that followed, and I knew that tongues must be wagging because I caught the Lush Gang eyeing them knowingly, but any speculation of what might or might not be happening between Bron and Jack was entirely eclipsed by a spectacular piece of scandal.

It was a Thursday breaktime when Tony Birch told me.

'Heard the latest?' he said.

'That all depends on what it is,' I said.

'Katie Fairlight's pregnant,' said Tony.

I said, 'Goodness! I wonder what caused that? Can I guess who the father is?'

'I bet Bryan's well pissed off!' said Tony.

'I'm sure it's just the initial shock,' I said. 'I hope he and Katie will be really, really happy.'

Tony believed I meant it and gave me The Look.

I though it was delicious news, but Bron's reaction was surprising.

'The silly cow!' she said when I told her. 'How could she be so irresponsible?'

'I don't think Katie deserves all the blame,' I said. 'I have a sneaking suspicion that Bryan may have had something to do with it as well.'

Bron was too angry to hear jokes. 'She's used the baby to trap him,' she said. 'When it's born, neither of them will want it.'

'Never mind,' I said. 'One day the baby will inherit the Eaves family fortune. With any luck it will inherit its mother's brains as well, and be too stupid to be unhappy.'

At the time, I couldn't quite understand why Bron was too angry to see the funny side of it, but things became a lot clearer the following Sunday.

I was washing up after lunch when the front-door bell chimed. I didn't go to the door myself, because I was wearing a pair of rather fetching pink rubber-gloves and I was afraid whoever had come calling might be inflamed by the sight of me in them. After a minute or two, Mother came into the kitchen.

She said, 'Wayne, your friend Bronia is here. I left her in the lounge with your father.'

I said, 'Well I hope you've been putting bromide in his tea, because it's the Winter Rut.'

I said this to cover up the fact that I was alarmed. Bron had never been to my house while my parents were in it before. She'd seen them in the street, or at Parents' Evenings at school, but she'd never observed them in their natural habitat.

When I got to the lounge I saw that Bron was anxious about something – I could tell

from the way she chewed her bottom lip. I
also saw that her unexpected appearance had
precipitated Father's male menopause. His
face was flushed and he was hopping about in
front of the sherry decanter like a demented
flamingo.

'Ah, Wayne!' he said. 'Your friend's here.'

'Why so she is!' I said.

'You should have told us she was coming!'
said Father.

'Why?' I said. 'Would you have slipped into
your silk dressing-gown?'

'But I haven't got a—!' said Father, then he
frowned and sighed deeply. 'Would you like a
sherry, Bronia?' he said.

'That's very kind of you, Mr Taylor, but it's
a bit early in the day for me,' said Bron. 'I just
popped in on impulse to see if Wayne wanted
to go for a walk.'

Father grunted appreciatively – he approved
of females having whims – and then Bron
finished him off with a smile that made him
spill sherry over his wrist.

It was freezing that afternoon. The wind
burned our faces with cold and we walked
with our arms round one another for warmth.
I could feel an edginess in Bron's shoulders.

'What's wrong?' I said.

'Jack,' said Bron.

I said, 'Oh?' but I'd been expecting it.

Bron said, 'I really like him – I mean, I liked
him the first time I met him. I think if he
hadn't been going out with Mikki . . .
Anyway, after the accident I started going to

see him because I thought he might need someone to talk to and . . .'

'He did,' I said.

Bron nodded and said, 'He feels so guilty about being alive. He feels everyone wishes that he'd died instead of Mikki.'

I didn't say anything. I couldn't; as far as I was concerned Jack was absolutely right.

Bron said, 'I wanted to be a friend to him, you know, he needed comforting and I needed comforting. Then, last weekend, it went a bit further than friendship.' She looked at me in a way that meant I didn't have to say anything. 'I know it was stupid, but it seemed right at the time. And now . . .'

'He wants to get serious,' I said.

'More serious than I want to get,' said Bron. 'More serious than I think I can be about anyone just at the moment. And anyway, I think he's using me to get over Mikki, you know? He's giving me all the feelings he can't give to her.'

'Does that surprise you?' I said.

'No,' said Bron, 'but *my* feelings do. It's like he's in the way. I've got to get over my own pain about Mikki and he's stopping me.'

I mulled it over. It was good mulling weather, and it was nearly dark enough to be evening, when you have to mull things over because nothing is clear. I understood now why Bron had been so upset by the news about Katie and Bryan. It was her own irresponsibility, not theirs, that had made her angry.

132

'What are you going to do?' I said finally.

I meant about Jack, but Bron misunderstood, or maybe she was deep inside herself and didn't hear.

'I'm going to be a doctor, Wayne,' she said. 'I want a job where I can help people and make a difference. It's because of what happened to Mikki. It feels like I owe it to her to do something important. Does that make sense?'

'Of course it does,' I said. 'It'll mean a lot of hard work though, won't it?'

'I know,' said Bron. 'I'm going to work hard and I'm not going to let anything or anyone get in my way.'

I said, 'When did you decide all this?'

Bron said, 'Now.'

It made me think how many things I still had to decide about myself, and when I was going to get around to doing something about them.

And that night, I had my first dream about Mikki since the accident.

In the dream, I was at school in the Design Studio. A lesson had just finished and everyone else had gone, but I was still packing away my things. I heard a footstep and I looked up, and there was Mikki in the doorway.

She said, 'Don't even *think* about leaving the room until you've spoken to me!'

And then she bounced over to me and gave me a hug.

'I really miss you,' she said.

25

I don't know if Bron had a heart-to-heart with Jack, but after she talked to me that Sunday he seemed to back off. He had a string of girl-friends while he was in the Sixth Form, though it was obvious that every time he looked at Bron he was seeing in moonlight. He wasn't the only one. Once she'd made up her mind about her future, Bron radiated a kind of determination and drive that made her very attractive. When you talked to her, you knew you were talking to someone who knew where she was going, and more than one person longed for her to take them with her.

I knew she still had fears and doubts because she talked them through with me, but to the other Sixth-Formers she was Bronia Arnold, Girl Wonder; and as far as most of the males were concerned she was Bronia the Unattainable. When she was made Head Girl at the end of the first year Sixth, no one was surprised and almost everybody seemed pleased. Mikki would have been proud of her . . .

Suzanne continued to talk to me at moments of crisis, which grew more numerous as her love-life became increasingly rococo. I actually enjoyed playing big brother and I gave her lots of wise advice which, being a sensible sort of person, she completely ignored.

And I went for it. I became absorbed in my studies and I worked my butt off. My Art work developed as painting stopped being just a way of showing people I was different and turned into a way of being.

My parents and I maintained an uneasy truce. There were no major battles, though there were skirmishes and the sniping was constant. Mother said I had a waspish wit, Father said I was just plain bloody-minded; they were both right.

In the Christmas term of the Upper Sixth, Bron directed the school production and she talked me into designing the set. I had a lot of guidance from Mr Trevor about my designs and he gave up a lot of his time to help me paint the set once it was built.

One Saturday morning, we were in the Main Hall, taking a break from painting a flat, when Mr Trevor said, 'It's very you, you know, Wayne.'

I blinked and wondered if he might be complimenting me on how well I looked in a paint-spattered boiler suit.

'What is?' I said.

Mr Trevor said, 'This design. The reds and greens – there's a lot of unresolved tension in it.'

While he rolled a cigarette, I stared at the set and tried to see what he meant.

'Is there?' I said.

Mr Trevor said, 'Yes, and there's a lot of unresolved tension in you. You ought to do something about it.'

'How?' I said. 'By visiting a massage-parlour?'

'By finding out who you are,' said Mr Trevor.

It was a perceptive remark and an alarming one, because I thought I'd made such a good job of being inscrutable.

'And how would I do that?' I said.

'Get out of this place for a start,' said Mr Trevor.

I said, 'I'm working at it. When I get to university—'

'I don't mean that,' Mr Trevor said. 'I mean travel. See a bit of the world. Find out what you want to go to university for.'

I thought I knew the answer to that one. I said, 'To find out more about Art.'

Mr Trevor said, 'Art isn't about university, it's about life.'

It was a tarnished old cliché, but for the first time I grasped what it meant. I'd been born and gone to school, and now I was planning to go to university, which was another kind of school. When I came out I'd know a lot about education and nothing about life at all.

I said, 'The world's a big place. I wouldn't know where to begin travelling.'

Mr Trevor said, 'That's a cop-out!'

136

And it was; he'd seen through me again and I was irritated.

I said, 'All right then, where would you go if you were me?'

Mr Trevor was seated on the edge of the stage and his legs were dangling down into the well of the hall, but all of a sudden he was somewhere else. His face looked different.

'I've got a friend in Greece,' he said. 'Nikos. Nikos Kolakis. He owns a restaurant called the Taverna Aphrodite . . .'

And he talked about the island. He talked about the village and the people, the mountains, and the heat, and the colour of the sea.

'But the best part is the night,' he said. 'You can walk away from the streetlights and go up the mountain and the moon's bright enough to cast shadows . . .'

He came back from the island with a shrug and a shake of his head.

I didn't; I stayed in his words and his words stayed in me.

During Easter term I was called for an interview at Sheffield. During the course of the interview, I just happened to wonder out loud what the attitude was to students who took a year out before starting their studies.

'We approve,' said the tutor. 'So many students go on to higher education without really knowing if it's what they want. It often turns out that they went to university because their parents and teachers put them under pressure, and they don't last the course.'

Those words stayed in me as well.

On the day I finished school and started study leave, I went to see Mr Trevor. He was teaching a noisy Year Eight group.

'I came to say thank you,' I said.

'That's all right,' said Trevor. 'It's my job.'

He broke off to savage two boys who were flicking paint at one another.

I meant to tell him how important he'd been to me, and how much I'd been shaped by his encouragement and criticism, but I could see that he was busy encouraging and criticising my successors, so I just said, 'Well, goodbye then,' which was lame, but appropriate.

Mr Trevor handed me a piece of paper.

'What's this?' I said.

'The address and phone number of my mate in Greece,' said Mr Trevor. 'He rang me the other night. If you fancy a job in his taverna, give him a call.'

'What, just like that?' I said.

'Just like that,' Mr Trevor said. 'Nikos is a really laid-back guy.'

I said, 'But—!'

'It's up to you, Wayne,' said Mr Trevor. 'It's always up to you – remember that.'

I said, 'Thanks.'

He said, 'Good luck.'

And we both spoke as if we really meant it.

26

The day my A levels finished, I wanted to celebrate but I had no one to celebrate with. Bron still had two exams to go and I knew she was up to her eyes in revision. I phoned Jack's number to see if he fancied going out somewhere, but there was no reply. In the end, I celebrated on my own and in my own way.

I phoned Nikos.

Mr Trevor was right about Nikos being very laid-back; he was also very charming. I figured that someone who could be charming on a phone a thousand miles away was probably worth meeting, and by the time I finished the call, I'd made my mind up about what I was going to do. The euphoria lasted for the rest of the following minute, and then I remembered that I'd have to tell my parents.

Waiting for them to get in from work was one of the longest waits I've ever known. I ran the conversation through in my imagination a dozen times, and the best one ended with my father ripping up my birth certificate and my mother taking an overdose of fabric conditioner. My ~~only~~ hope lay in the ~~fact that~~ Mother always came home first. With a little work and some sparkling verbal gymnastics, I might just be able to convince her and have her on my side by the time father got in.

I went up to my room and listened to music. When I heard a car pull up in the drive I rushed downstairs and ran straight into Father.

I said, 'What are you doing here?'

Father said, 'I live here.'

I said, 'I mean, what are you doing home so early?'

Father said, 'I'm not early. I just left work on time for once.'

I was so thrown that I engaged Father in small-talk – very small talk.

I must have tried to tell them about fifty times over dinner, but every time I opened my mouth, Father snarled something about work and Mother made mewing noises to keep him pacified.

We were half-way through the chocolate mousse with kiwi fruit when Father suddenly said, 'Exams all over, eh, Wayne?'

'Yes,' I said.

'Going out on the town?' said Father.

'No,' I said. 'I was thinking of just going wild and having a second helping of dessert.'

Father parried this with a rattle of his spoon.

'You'd better get a job for the summer,' he said. 'You're going to need plenty of savings when you start university.'

'I've got a job,' I said.

'Ah!' said Father. 'Toynbee, Charles and Wooton?'

I said, 'No. Actually, I thought I might have a change this summer.'

'Oh?' said Father.

I said, 'I'm going to work as a waiter in a taverna on one of the Greek islands. I'm going out at the beginning of August and working through until the end of the tourist season in November. I'm not sure what I'll do after that. I might come back to Britain and get a job, or I might travel on from Greece if I've saved enough.'

The silence that followed wasn't so much stony as diamond-hard. I took a spoonful of mousse and it felt like a dead jellyfish in my mouth.

Father had gone completely frog – all bulging eyes and twitching throat.

'But what—?' he said. 'But you—? But what about university?'

'They're going to keep a place open for me next year,' I said.

Father said, 'What the devil d'you think you're playing at?'

'Life,' I said.

'You don't know the first thing about it,' said Father.

'Time I found out, then,' I said.

Father spluttered a few times and then stopped, like a recalcitrant motor-mower.

Mother reacted differently. Mother was cool, with a Mona Lisa smile and distant eyes.

'Greece!' she said softly. 'How exciting!'

141

'Exciting?' said Father. 'Hare-brained is more like it! I thought you were settling down, Wayne. I mean, you've got a place at university, a career to aim at, a steady girlfriend—'

'No I haven't,' I said.

'What about Bronia?' said Father.

I said, 'Bronia's not my girlfriend. I'm not interested in having a girlfriend.'

Father was litmus-paper pink.

'Then what are you interested in?' he said.

'Me,' I said. 'I want to find out more about me! Haven't you ever really wanted to do something?'

Father dabbed his lips with his napkin.

'I wanted to have a comfortable home,' he said. 'I wanted a decent, normal family life.'

'Well welcome to the real world, Father,' I said.

Father's face froze, and then thawed. There were slack lines around his mouth and something I didn't recognise in his eyes, though I realise now that it was pain. When he spoke, his voice was calm and small.

'I don't understand you,' he said. 'I've tried and tried to understand you, but I can't. Why is that?'

I couldn't tell him. We'd never understood one another, we'd only reacted. I looked at him and tried to find me in his face, and I saw that he was trying to find himself in mine.

Mother said, 'Well, I think Wayne is being very brave.'

Father and I turned to stare at her. I don't know which of us was more amazed.

Mother said, 'Instead of following the rest of the flock, Wayne's striking out on his own. I wish I'd had the nerve to be different and break free when I was his age. If I had, I might not spend so much time regretting the things I haven't done.'

There was a determined set to Mother's jaw and I suddenly noticed that her nose was the same shape as mine, and our eyes were the same colour. It made me feel odd.

Father said, 'Gwen?'

Mother said, 'Gordon, Wayne's eighteen. He can leave home any time he wants to – it's up to him. What's up to us is whether he leaves feeling bitter about us, or feeling that we've tried to meet him half-way.' She carefully set her spoon in her dish and stood up. 'And now I'm going to make some coffee,' she said.

After Mother left the room, Father went on gazing at her chair as though she were still in it.

I said, 'I'm sorry this has come as a shock to you, Father . . . It's not your fault . . . I didn't mean to—'

Father said, 'Tell me something, Wayne.'

'What?' I said.

Father said, 'Why do you always call me Father? You've never called me Daddy, or Dad – it's always been Father.'

'Well,' I said, 'Dad always seemed so informal.'

Father looked at me. I expected him to bluster, or even explode, but instead he took me completely by surprise. He laughed until he had to dry his eyes with his napkin.

He said, 'Listen, Wayne, all I ever wanted was—' He stopped and shook his head. 'No,' he said, 'it'll keep. I'd better go and give your mother a hand.'

And that's the evening my father and I reached, if not an understanding, then at least a new level of misunderstanding.

27

There were forms to be filled in, of course. Then travel arrangements had to be made, which meant filling in more forms. I did it without thinking, which was best, because if I stopped to think I had a terrible impulse to be frivolous and write: SEX: Hmm! MARITAL STATUS: Available.

I wonder if you have to fill in forms to apply for a job designing forms for other people to fill in?

After a week or so of this, I was at screaming point. All I wanted to do was get on a plane and go, but the frustration was good because it stopped me having second thoughts.

The night before I left, I went out with Bron, Jack and Emma, his latest girlfriend. Emma was in the Lower Sixth and hadn't been going out with Jack very long. She was plainly awed at being in the company of Sixth Form legends, because she hardly said a word. We went to the Duke – where else? – and talked; or rather Jack and I traded bad jokes while Bron groaned and Emma smiled vacantly.

At one point, Jack and I visited the Gents to return our beer to the water cycle, and Jack said, 'I'm going to miss you, Wayne.'

I said, 'Are you?'

Jack said, 'When we first met, I thought you and I were going to be really close mates, but then . . . well . . .'

'Mikki,' I said.

Jack said, 'Yes. Look, Emma and I aren't – I mean, I wouldn't want you to think it was anything like . . .' He shook his head as though he had something stuck in his hair. 'D'you ever think you see her?' he said.

I said, 'Who?'

Jack said, 'Mikki. I do. Sometimes when I'm walking down the street, I'll see someone and just for a second I think it's her and my insides go all . . .' He shook his head again. 'She was so amazing. When am I ever going to find anyone like her again?'

I said, 'You can't change what's happened, Jack. All you can do is get on with what you've got. Wanting to go back is a crime.'

I thought – Well, get me! Wayne, the Wise Old Man of the Mountains!

Jack said, 'If I give you my address, will you write to me?'

I said, 'I promise to send you a series of the most obscene postcards I can find.'

Jack smiled and grunted and said, 'I'm sorry. I really am.'

I didn't need to ask what he was talking about, and if I'd told him not to be silly or that it didn't matter, I would have been lying, so I didn't say anything.

It broke up quite early: Jack and Emma wanted time alone together and I didn't want to start my new life with a hangover. Bron and I caught the bus, and when it passed the place where the accident had happened, she grabbed my hand and squeezed it hard.

I said, 'I'm glad you're coming to see me off tomorrow. I can't think of anyone better for my parents to drive back with.'

'Why?' said Bron.

'Because you'll be kind to them.'

Bron said, 'What if you make lots of new friends and—?'

I said, 'I can't go away from you Bron. We're scarred in the same places.'

After I'd walked her home, I didn't go straight back to my house. I emancipated my feet and followed where they took me, and they took me to Northmeadows School playground.

It was a clear night and the moon was up. I stood on the edge of the playground and stared at the climbing frame, and thought about Mikki. After a while, I said, 'I'm going to try hard to be honest and angry. I'll try not to waste any time. I'm not leaving you here, you're coming with me, inside. You're why I'm doing this, after all.'

I don't know why I spoke out loud, because I knew she wasn't there. I was only speaking to the playground, the dark and the moonlight, and it made me feel foolish, so I turned away and walked home.

Next morning, Heathrow was a nightmare. Thick caterpillars of queues undulated towards the checking-in desks and I was so nervous I felt increasingly as though I might lay an egg at any moment. Father passed so many helpful remarks about how different things would have been if I'd travelled business class instead of economy that I sent him off with Bron and Mother in search of coffee.

This wasn't altogether a good idea, because once I was alone, I began to wonder. Was this really a good idea? Was I doing the right thing? When I found out that I didn't know, it came as a real relief.

After I got my boarding-pass, I found my parents and Bron seated at the table of a fast-food bar. Bron smiled at me reassuringly, while Mother and Father plied me with questions.

– Yes, I was being met at the airport on the island.

– No, I hadn't forgotten my Greek currency.

– Of course, I would ring them when I arrived.

My flight was called. We moved to the departure gate and the moment I'd been dreading.

Bron hugged me tight. I closed my eyes, and I was in New Place, Mikki's kitchen and Heathrow Airport all at the same time.

Bron said, 'I love you, Wayne. There isn't enough time not to tell you.'

I said, 'You know I love you too, so it's all right.'

Then Mother hugged me and said, 'Be happy.'

And then I turned to Father, and that was what I'd been dreading most because I didn't know what to do.

Father was fiddling with a piece of paper.

'I've been meaning to get some extra bits and bobs for the computer,' he said, 'but then I thought—'

He handed me the paper. It was the stub of a Lloyd's Bank paying-in slip, written out in Father's small, neat hand. He'd paid five hundred pounds into my bank account.

Father said, 'Just in case, you know. Emergencies and whatnot.'

I looked at the stub and it made me want to cry. I looked at my father and thought of all the time we'd spent struggling with one another. Now he was helping me to do something he disapproved of. The stub was a sign that he'd accepted I was a different person from the one he'd thought I was, or wanted me to be.

In return, I gave him the only thing I had to give.

I said, 'Thanks, Dad.'

And I came here, to the Taverna Aphrodite, the village, the mountains, the heat like the roar of a lion, and the balcony where I'm writing now. The difference of it all staggered me at first – even the plants and the insects were different. I couldn't get over cucumbers growing wild at the sides of the road and the huge bumblebees the colour of tar. I couldn't get over the fact that some evenings the mountains looked as pink as seaside-rock.

Mostly, I couldn't get over fitting in. Nikos treated me like a friend from day one, and the other waiters started insulting me at once. Insults are the currency you use to buy acceptance in the taverna. The place flowed around me as accommodatingly as an amoeba ingesting a diatom.

Being on my own has taught me things. I still hurt about Mikki, but I know now that you can't cry people out of the dark, or call them back by saying their names, and you can't be with them in words. I've written it all down, and I've found that words don't smile and they can't give you a hug.

Sometimes when I wake up, I think I can hear her talking and laughing. I get this crazy idea that if I get out of bed and go outside I'll see her, walking up the road between the shadows of the carob trees, wearing her total grin . . .

I've learned some other things, too.

The third week in August, in the middle of a horrendously busy lunchtime with the taverna stiff with exacting German tourists, my parents rang to tell me my exam results. It was a difficult phone-call: the line was bad, so I had to bawl, and I got confused between A-levels and A grades. When the message finally got through that I had two As and a D, I was too hoarse to feel elated, but something must have shown on my face, because when I put the phone down, Nikos said, 'Is good news, Wayne?'

I said, 'I've passed my exams.'

Nikos said, 'Good. Then tomorrow night I take off and you come with me. I take you where I go to eat.'

And he did. He left the taverna to Georgiou and the other waiters and drove me down the coast to a little fishing village. The taverna we ate at had tables set out under a canvas awning at the edge of a rocky beach. We chose our fish from the kitchen and then we sat outside, drinking cool wine and watching evening come down over the bay. Nikos translated Greek jokes into English so successfully that some of them made me laugh.

After we'd eaten, Nikos lit a cigarette and looked at me. He said, 'Wayne, you are what? You like girls, you like boys, what?'

If anyone else had asked me anywhere else, I would have been flip, but I knew Nikos wasn't asking me so that he could poke fun, he was genuinely curious.

'Yes,' I said. 'I like girls, I like boys.'

Nikos shrugged with his shoulders and his mouth.

'Then how come you don't go with someone?' he said.

I said, 'Because if I go with someone, I might have to do something, and the idea of doing anything puts me off. It's all so sordid.'

Nikos frowned at 'sordid' so I said, 'Dirty.'

Nikos drew circles in the air with his cigarette, trying to spin words up to the top of his memory.

'No,' he said. 'Is nothing dirty. When you meet the right person, is everything beautiful.'

I said, 'But I haven't met the right person yet. I'm waiting until I can see in moonlight.'

Nikis said, 'This, I don't understand.'

I said, 'No. Neither do I.'

Now it's October and sometimes the wind blows from Africa. It's a peculiar wind, because it doesn't do what you expect – standing in it makes you hotter, not cooler. It's a dry, dirty wind and it comes suddenly, blowing off the tourists' sun hats and upsetting the tidy racks of postcards outside the minimarkets. I hate that wind, but it excites me. Maybe when the season's over, I'll go where it comes from . . .

Meanwhile, there are other things for me to think about – like Bron.

I've had a lot of letters from her. She's in university now, and she's met someone called David. When she writes about him, she sounds more and more fraught, and I sense that she's struggling with herself. The last letter I got from her ended:

I must talk to you. I've got to see you. It doesn't do anything but rain here and it's driving me mad! I want to sit in the sun and talk to you until everything makes sense. Can I? If I come to see you, will I be in the way?

I've had a lot of letters from Suzanne too, and I gather that she and Bron have been in contact, because in *her* last letter, she put:

Bron says she's coming to see you. It's all right for her, but I'm stuck here where it's so POOEY!!

But W-a-a-a-y-n-e, if I nag and make a fuss and sulk until Mum and Dad say yes, can I come and see you too?

I laughed when I read this, but then I remembered how well Suzanne can nag, and make a fuss, and sulk, and it made me worried.

I've got the room, of course, as long as I sleep on a lounger in the kitchen. There'll be lots of bawdy comments at the taverna, but I can handle it . . .

I don't believe for a moment that either of them will get over here, but in idle moments I wonder about it. I see the three of us together, and I see Bron and I desperately trying to turn Suzanne into Mikki so we can have the Great Triangle back again. That wouldn't be fair – Suzanne's worth more than that.

When I have those thoughts, I know I ought to write back and say no to them both, but then, when I'm reaching for my pen, I see it all differently.

The taxi will drop them at the bottom of the steps leading up to the taverna. I'll be waiting at the top of the steps, underneath the mulberry tree, and I'll be smiling – Wayne the Charmer, Wayne the Understander, Big Brother Wayne. And there won't be any pressure on Suzanne to be someone else.

Bron and I will be Mikki.